'You're an interesting paradox, you know. Ice maiden, with fiery red hair, simmering green eyes and a soft vulnerable smile. . .'

'Look,' she burst out, goaded beyond control, 'I thought you suggested a truce earlier?'

'I hadn't realised I was resuming hostilities!' Guy pointed out blithely. 'I'm just interested to know what goes on beneath that hostile little shell you present to the world, Virginia. Why do you find that so threatening, I wonder?'

Books you will enjoy
by ROSALIE ASH

PRIVATE PROPERTY

When Henrietta finally accepted Nick Trevelyan's wonderful job offer, she didn't need to hear his previous secretary's warning about the folly of falling in love with her dark, brooding boss. But Nick seemed bent on taking possession of her—and how much longer would she be able to resist his kisses?

THE GYPSY'S BRIDE

Saul Gallagher's unexpected return into Chessy's life brought with it a host of bitter emotions she would have given anything not to feel again. Oh, the wild streak of gypsy had been replaced by a sleek sophistication, but he was just as arrogant and ready to condemn her. So why was he suddenly so interested in Chessy?

LOVE BY DESIGN

BY
ROSALIE ASH

MILLS & BOON LIMITED
ETON HOUSE   18–24 PARADISE ROAD
RICHMOND   SURREY   TW9 1SR

First published in Great Britain 1991
by Mills & Boon Limited

© Rosalie Ash 1991

Australian copyright 1991
Philippine copyright 1992
This edition 1992

ISBN 0 263 77403 1

Set in 10 on 12 pt Linotron Baskerville
01-9201-51356
Typeset in Great Britain by Centracet, Cambridge
Made and printed in Great Britain

CHAPTER ONE

'I JUST don't understand.' Virginia switched her disconcertingly direct aquamarine gaze from her father's haggard face to her brother Charles's preoccupied gloom, finishing up on her sister-in-law Lucy's flushed, anxious expression. 'I mean, I realise I'm the *baby* of the family, *and* a mere *female*——' the latter drew a bleak smile from her father, acknowledging a point of contention between them spanning several years '—but I don't see how just a *fire* can mean the end of everything! Surely——'

'Dad didn't say it was the end of everything, Virgie. . .' Charles cut in gently. 'Three years at college hasn't changed your habit of exaggeration, has it?'

'Don't try and sidetrack me. . .' Virginia pushed agitated hands through her hair, forgetting it was caught up neatly in a high top-knot. The result was several more escaped strands of red-gold framing the pale oval beauty of her face. 'And please don't patronise me! This board of directors has just been spelling out the fact that we're in big trouble; we're heavily in debt, we're showing a. . .a net loss before taxation. . .we can barely afford this month's wages bills, we can't meet half our orders. . .all that doesn't just come blazing in overnight after an accident with the new *singeing* machine in the printing plant. . .'

'No,' her father agreed heavily, green eyes, a paler version of Virginia's, clouding with pain. 'It comes, I'm afraid, from a rather out-dated style of management, a

5

lack of innovation, and poor market research. . .the bank's description, I hasten to add, not mine——'

'And a rocky economy and prohibitive interest rates!' Charles protested quickly, hurt at the slight on his role as sales and design director of Sarah Chester Fabrics.

'However we describe it, and I blame myself as much as anyone else, Charles, believe me, we need some heavy investment, quite apart from the insurance money. . .to keep afloat. The bank require "a fresh voice" in the management before they'll bail us out.'

'Which is where Guy Sterne, Charles's yuppie friend from the City, fits into the picture, I presume?' Virginia said with quiet distaste, gazing round the old mahogany boardroom table, infuriatingly aware that her family were mentally shrugging their shoulders at her protests. The boardroom was half empty now, just the Chester family remaining following the break-up of the emergency board meeting a few minutes earlier.

'Guy is not a yuppie,' Charles remonstrated, in the voice he reserved for humouring his little sister when she was being most irritating, 'He just happens to be a very successful. . .' her brother hesitated a fraction as if searching for the most appropriate description '. . .*entrepreneur*.'

'Out to make a fast buck! Grandma would have a fit if she was alive! Believe me, a man like that won't give a damn about the ideals Gran established. . .about caring for the welfare of the workforce, about. . .about the *morality* of labour. . .and besides, he won't be remotely interested in the textile industry!'

Charles and her father exchanged glances. A lock of straight chestnut-brown hair flopped over her brother's high, idealistic forehead, and he smiled his crooked, boyish smile at her.

'Profit is profit, whatever the industry.' The cynicism was rare, coming from Charles's lips, and Virginia felt the cold hand of reality gripping her. It was true, it *must* be true, then. Chester's really *was* in deep trouble. . .

'So out of the window will fly all the ideals Sarah Chester Fabrics has stood for?'

'If we don't persuade someone like Guy to help us out, there won't *be* a Sarah Chester Fabrics, never mind the ideals!'

Charles always smiled like that when he wanted to appease her. But Virginia felt a surge of frustration. How many times had Charles and her father put her down, discounted her opinions?

If it weren't for the fact that her grandmother had helped her grandfather form the original company of Sarah Chester Fabrics, that it was her grandmother's designs combined with her grandfather's technical know-how that had started the whole thing off, she'd have written off all the Chester males as hopeless chauvinists. As it was, despite the company's bearing her grandmother's name, Dad and Charles always treated her lightly, conveyed the impression that the sooner she was married and having babies, like Lucy, the better! It was just so unfair!

Past injustices began to smart all over again, and she felt annoyed with herself for being so self-centred at a time when the family firm appeared to be teetering towards bankruptcy. But Dad had always given responsibility to Charles, shared his worries and fears with Charles. . .well, that was fine, as long as she was allowed her fair say as well. But she wasn't. Oh, admittedly, she was younger. Still only twenty-one. And she'd been nicknamed 'Scatty' because of a habit of daydreaming her way through the mundane bits of life. But a childhood gaining a reputation as an impulsive scatterbrain shouldn't preclude her from the same opportunities and privileges her brother received, should it? Academically she'd always held her own. If her results were good in August, she *might* even be able to boast a BA Hons in textile design. Why should it have to be so *difficult* to be taken seriously?

'So we have to hand over the reins of Chester's to a man whose only interest is money for money's sake?' she persisted in a low, intense voice, 'when anyone can see all the company needs is a re-think of direction, a bit of diversification. . .'

'Credit your brother and me with a little intelligence, Virginia.' Her father's voice was cold, and he stood up abruptly, his gaze sweeping dismissively over them all. 'If there'd been a way to avoid this mess, we're experienced enough in the business to have spotted it!'

Virginia bit her lip, caught Lucy's placatory smile, and took a deep breath.

'Yes. Of course.' It was a low, bitter retort, and she was gradually becoming aware that the intensity of the scene had brought on another of those infuriating headaches.

'Go home with Lucy and get some rest, and don't worry your pretty head about the business,' her father added with a slightly guilty air, as if suddenly recalling her convalescent status. 'You look as white as a ghost, Ginny, darling.'

'Just temper, Daddy, darling,' she muttered under her breath, her anger threatening to bubble to the surface, only failing to do so because of the sickening throb in her forehead. Lucy, easing the temporary bulk of her stomach out from behind the table, stood up as well.

'Tea, in the conservatory, I think. Don't you, Virgie?'

'Good idea.' Virginia held the office door open for Charles's very pregnant wife, and smiled a cool goodbye to the men behind them. 'See you later.'

Out in the car park, Lucy handed over the car keys to Virginia and wedged herself into the passenger-seat, glancing rather apprehensively at Virginia as they accelerated slightly too fast out of the car park.

In a few minutes they'd left behind the head office of Chester Fabrics, driven past the fire-blackened fabric printing plant and escaped into the lush green countryside on the way back to Armscott Manor, the rambling Cotswold home of the Chesters for three generations. It was hard to believe it was nearly August. A glimmer of sun, the first they'd seen for days in a chillier than average English summer, was gilding the meadow-sweet creamy-white in the tangled hedgerows. Its sensuous aroma drifted in through the open sun-roof, provoking a little series of painful memories of country walks in Oxfordshire with Mortimer. . . It had been quite a year, in more ways than one. . .

They'd driven several miles before Lucy finally ventured, 'Try not to let it get under your skin, Virgie.'

Virginia realised she'd been gripping the steering-wheel unnecessarily tightly and consciously relaxed, forcing a laugh and wincing as the vibration worsened her headache. 'I don't usually. But it's so frustrating. I've got shares in the company, but no one thinks to let me know when it's sinking without trace!'

'You were away at college. You'd been ill. We all

thought you could do without extra worries. Besides, until the fire, no one really knew how bad things had got. . .'

'But it's the way Dad and Charles just. . .just *humour* me. When I *know* I could make valuable contributions to the business. . .'

'I know you've taken a degree in textile design. . .' Lucy sounded hesitant as Virginia turned down the long curving drive of the house, pulled the estate car into the shade of the cedar tree and cut the engine. 'But Charles says the bank wants new, strong management. He's not exactly thrilled at the prospect himself. So——'

'So a twenty-one-year-old design graduate from Central School of Art is *not* what the bank are looking for?' Virginia supplied wryly, climbing out of the car and helping Lucy out. 'Yes, I know that! I'm *not* looking for some sinecure of a job with the cosy family firm, Lucy! I'm more than willing to carve my own career— I'm raring to go, at least I shall be *if* I get my degree and *if* I can shake off this horrible *mononucleosis*, as Dr Newne pompously insists on calling it! Come on, I'll make the tea. You look as if you could do with collapsing on a sofa.'

'I'm not sure which of us is in worse condition at the moment!' Lucy said ruefully, gratefully lowering herself on to a floral-cushioned, wicker-backed sofa in the conservatory and reluctantly submitting to Virginia's fussing with a footstool, 'Is Mrs Chalk still there? I bet she'd rustle up a tray of tea if you smile at her nicely!'

'I'll go and see. Whatever you do, don't move!'

Virginia went slowly through the conservatory, through the cool, tiled rear lobby, and into the kitchen. Mrs Chalk was nowhere to be found, so she made straight for the medicine cupboard in the spacious Georgian-style kitchen with its enormous, old-fashioned white-painted cupboards and scrubbed-elm table, and located the painkillers, swallowing the dosage with water before setting about making the tea. The after-effects of a severe bout of glandular fever were beginning to linger on far too long for Virginia's liking. Always used to a high energy level, she had found that the need over the last few months to pace herself, rest, keep calm, was driving her slowly insane.

'Aren't you and Charles due to go off on holiday soon?' she queried, when tea and biscuits were duly dispensed to Lucy and she could sit down on a wicker-backed chair and sip her own. 'I seem to recall an exotic Caribbean trip was booked up?'

'I've been meaning to talk to you about that.' Lucy leaned further back on the sofa, and took a thoughtful drink of her tea. 'We can't go.'

'Oh, Lucy!' Virginia's green eyes clouded in dismay. She sat forward on the chair, studying her sister-in-law's face with a worried frown. 'But you were looking forward to it so much! Is it because of the baby? Or the crisis in the factory?'

Lucy pulled a rueful face.

'A bit of both. Charles couldn't leave Dad to face it all alone. But it seems I've been a bit blasé about pregnancy's being "a perfectly natural physical state"—dear Dr Newne hit his surgery roof when I casually mentioned flying to St Lucia! Apparently even if I was within the time limit of twenty-eight weeks' pregnancy—which of course I'm not—I couldn't possibly stand an eight-hour flight; I've got a *touch* of toxaemia——'

'Lucy! You featherbrain! Surely you checked limits on pregnancy and flying when you booked the holiday?'

Lucy gave an expansive shrug, and laughed. 'I confess I just didn't think. You know Charles only married me because he wanted a dizzy blonde to boost his ego!'

Virginia groaned, then sobered, gazing in real concern at her sister-in-law.

'Toxaemia? That sounds tricky—shouldn't you be in hospital or something?'

The other girl's blue eyes shone in amusement. 'No, it's not quite that desperate.'

'Well, it certainly sounds it!'

'Don't fuss. Pregnancy is a perfectly natural physical state, remember? I'm not allowed to go jetting off to the Caribbean, that's all. Which brings me to my main point, Virgie. Charles and I want you to go instead!'

'Me?' Virginia's jaw dropped open in surprise. She stared at Lucy, sea-green eyes wide with conflicting feelings. 'That's a ridiculous idea. . .'

'Why? You definitely need a holiday. After battling through to the end of your course in London, and coming home looking like death warmed up——'

'Thanks!'

'—ten days on St Lucia, swimming around in the pellucid Caribbean waters——'

'Swimming in the *what*?' Virginia burst out, grinning.

'Just quoting the purple prose of the travel brochures,' Lucy laughed. 'Seriously, Virgie, love, do think about it. You owe it to yourself to get fit. . . Charles and I and your father are really worried about you, if you want the truth! You've lost so much weight, darling! I know your degree meant a lot to you, but in all honesty you might have been better resting for longer. . .'

'I couldn't just throw away all the work I'd already done!' Virginia protested. 'And frankly, I couldn't disappear to the West Indies and leave you all in this mess with the business.'

Lucy raised her eyebrows. 'No? What good can you do mooning around worrying, picking at your food like an anorexic, and giving yourself splitting headaches? If you're worried about Chester's, and you really think you could do something to help, a relaxing holiday should set you up for the fight!'

Virginia made a face. 'I must admit a fight is the *last* thing I feel like right now. I mean, mentally I feel angry, but physically I feel rather like a limp dish-rag! But a Caribbean holiday. . . I mean, I couldn't even begin to afford it!'

'Forget the cost. The villa's booked, the flights are booked—Charles can cancel his and I'll transfer mine over to your name. . .'

'I thought air tickets weren't transferable?' Virginia frowned, drawing on her limited knowledge of package tours and cheap flights.

'Only the APEX type. Our tickets are club class and you can do what you like with those. Will you just stop fretting and arguing and imagine ten days in the balmy tropical climate of the Eastern Caribbean Windward Isles? The trade winds blowing across thousands of miles of the Atlantic ocean providing perfect air-conditioning?' Lucy recited, in glowing mock travel-speak. 'Exactly what you need to banish the dreaded *mononucleosis* for ever! And Guy's villa is the ultimate in luxury; it overlooks Marigot Bay and it's got——'

'Guy's villa?' Virginia narrowed her eyes suddenly. 'Guy who?'

Catching a fleeting expression on Lucy's face, she persisted with ominous calm, 'This wouldn't be the Guy Sterne whose name we've just been dutifully worshipping at the board meeting, by any chance?'

'So what if it is?' Lucy, normally unflappable, sounded exasperated. 'What on earth does it matter *who* owns the villa?'

'It's the principle of the thing——'

'*Principle*!' Lucy said heatedly. 'Honestly, I don't know who's the most stubborn, you or your father! There's a villa vacant, and you've got the chance to take a well-earned holiday there. If you're going to be ridiculously pedantic about *principles*, as you call them, practically every private villa in existence is owned by somebody with loads of money—is that a good reason never to rent a villa?'

'OK, calm down. You shouldn't lose your temper in your condition!' Virginia countered with a wry grin at Lucy's flushed cheeks.

'Yes, but Virgie, what on earth have you got against this man? You haven't even met him.' Lucy stopped, glancing searchingly at her. '*Have* you?'

'Certainly not. And I've no wish to meet him. I simply can't stand whizz-kid City high-flyers who think of nothing but profit and loss accounts and their latest seven-series BMW and where their next magnum of Bollinger is coming from!'

'Guy's a friend of Charles's. He's also a very nice person.'

Lucy pushed her flaxen curls from her forehead, her reproving tone hinting that such open prejudice showed lamentable immaturity.

'Nice?' Virginia smoothed the soft folds of her flower-sprigged 'Sarah Chester' dress around her knees, fighting with her irrational flare of annoyance. 'I assume you're using the word "nice" in the true sense of "neat", as in the neatly ruthless deals I'm sure he's notorious for clinching, or the neat asset-stripping technique which I dare say he's renowned for?'

'Virgie, what *are* you talking about?'

'I'm talking about Guy Sterne, of Schreider Sterne Inc. Aren't you? I've heard their name mentioned by someone at college. This boy's uncle's firm ended up in the clutches of Guy Sterne's company, and they were *annihilated*!'

'That sounds like a *slight* exaggeration?' Lucy countered.

'Not at all. One minute the firm was having a few financial problems and hoping for some helpful invest-ment advice, the next their premises were sold off to a factory development corporation, their directors sacked, the workforce were redundant. Overnight they ceased to exist. And that's a typical kind of Guy Sterne oper-ation—the only goal is profit. He doesn't give a damn about the human beings he pushes around!'

'And that's only hearsay! You don't imagine Charles would have asked Guy to help us if he thought he was some kind of financial *shark*? You're just generalising. . .*wildly*!'

Virginia raised her eyes towards the ceiling. 'Lucy, darling, you may be a married, pregnant lady five years my senior, but I honestly wonder which of us is the most gullible and naïve!'

'It's not me who's invited Guy to bail the company

out of trouble, remember, it's Charles and your father. Are you saying they're gullible and naïve?'

Virginia stood up abruptly, taking a deep breath to control herself.

'No,' she said heavily. 'No, I suppose not.' Blinkered, old-fashioned; maybe, she added to herself, ripe for the kill. Did her family honestly imagine Guy Sterne's interest in Sarah Chester's would be purely altruistic? Motivated by a selfless desire to assist an ailing firm back on its feet, without interfering in its structure, its established systems?

But Lucy's blue eyes were so hurt that she felt a strong pang of shame. Charles's wife was warm-hearted, vulnerable even when she wasn't heavily pregnant.

'I'm sorry. I'm being foul at the moment. And I shouldn't be upsetting you.'

'Then you'll humour me, Virgie, and stop being such a doom-merchant? You'll take advantage of my air-ticket and go to St Lucia?' Lucy thrust in craftily.

'I'll think about it.' Catching Lucy's expression, she added with more emphasis, 'Really, I will.'

'You'd better! And if you refuse to go on the grounds of this silly prejudice against a man you haven't even met, just because you disapprove of the way he's made his money, that makes you a bigot, Virginia Chester! After all, the family is hardly on the breadline. We might have problems with the business, but Chester's has always had money, always been relatively well-off landowners, even before your grandparents began printing fabrics!'

Virginia pulled a face at her sister-in-law, but she was pensive as she leaned back in her chair and stared through the glass conservatory at the manicured lawns and high, shaven box hedges beyond. Suddenly she was beset with self-doubt. It was possible that ideals could sometimes get tangled up with prejudices. And, in her present dubious physical state, the prospect of a holiday of any description, let alone a luxury one in the West Indies, was undoubtedly an irresistible proposition. Even her emotions had taken a recent battering, she reflected wryly, with the unpleasant outcome of her relationship with Mortimer Harrison following not so very long after the shattering loss of her mother. . .

Two sources of emotional stability had been whipped from under her feet in relatively quick succession— though it was hardly right to compare them—her mother had been her best friend, her chief confidante, almost a soul-mate. Mortimer had betrayed trust of a different kind, in a very different way. . .after all, her mother's death had been a tragic stroke of fate. It wasn't very fair to feel betrayed by someone you loved, someone very close to you, simply because they'd had the misfortune to die suddenly. . .

'You needn't worry about Guy coming down to make any changes at Chester's while you're gone,' Lucy was adding calmly, as if sensing victory. 'He was just about to go away on business when Charles rang to tell him we weren't going to St Lucia after all. He won't be calling a meeting here for at least a fortnight.'

Virginia stared at her sister-in-law blankly.

'When were you due to fly?'

'Sunday. So you'd better start packing—don't forget a cagoule. The rainy season's just beginning.'

'I haven't said I'm going yet!'

'I know. But at least you've stopped arguing. That's

half the battle.' Lucy leaned back with an air of satisfaction, then dimpled a grin at Virginia, adding apologetically, 'Could you possibly pour me another cup of tea? This baby has gone into one of his frenetic football sessions and if I move it'll set him off again!'

Four days later, a bemused Virginia was sipping a glass of fresh orange juice on the terrace of Guy Sterne's isolated and undeniably stylish holiday villa.

It was late afternoon, she had to keep reminding herself, even though her body-clock seemed stubbornly convinced it was bedtime. And here she was, all in one piece, in St Lucia, one of the Windward Islands in the Caribbean Sea, breathing in seductive scents of unknown spices and blossoms on warm tropical air.

The question circling her head as she'd climbed aboard the BA 747 that morning was why on earth had she let herself be talked into this? But that was silly, because she knew why. Lucy's glowing descriptions of swaying palms and white beaches had disgracefully tipped the balance between a sense of duty, and a yearning for a spot of sheer, unadulterated pampering. Oh, it was true that Dad and Charles had joined forces with Lucy in a deafening chorus of encouragement, to such a degree that she'd felt almost piqued by their eagerness to be rid of her. But deep down she'd known she was sitting on a plane bound for the Caribbean because she wanted to be. In addition to art and history, travel of any kind had always been a powerful addiction. To be heading down towards the Equator, towards tiny islands in the sun where pirates and privateers must have taken refuge to lie in wait for those gold-laden Spanish galleons, where a rich mixture of French, Dutch,

Spanish and English had left an intriguing treasure-chest of cultures to be explored. . .

It wouldn't solve any problems back in England, of course. It wouldn't settle the shaky future of a family business painstakingly built up with love and commitment, it wouldn't alter the shock of Mortimer's twisted values. . .but it would definitely take her mind off it all for a while.

But now she was here there was so much to assimilate, and she felt impatient at being so unfit. She longed to rid herself of this infuriating tiredness and start exploring everything. . . She blinked exhausted eyes at the view before her, struggling against the fatigue which had begun at Gatwick and increased steadily throughout the journey. The heat was intense, humid. She was gradually becoming conscious of aches and pains caused by the long, tiring flight and the horrendously bumpy drive from the airport to Marigot Bay.

'Did you say this was the *main* road?' she'd felt compelled to ask, as they'd zigzagged and ricocheted off massive pot-holes at what felt like Brands Hatch speed. Her driver was a tall, friendly man called Noble Soloman, with one of the most infectious laughs she'd ever heard. His vehicle was called a taxi, but Virginia had privately questioned whether a bright orange mini-van, lined with fake tiger fur and blaring non-stop earsplitting calypso music, could rightfully claim that title.

'Sure is! This is the main West Coast Highway.'

'I'd hate to experience a St Lucian cart-track.' She'd smiled with gritted teeth. 'But this is a beautiful island!' she'd added, in deference to the unmistakable note of pride in the man's voice.

'We say St *Loo-sha*,' the driver had explained, picking up her mistaken pronunciation. 'The Helen of the West Indies! The English and French fought over her like the Greeks and Romans fought over Helen of Troy!'

She could believe that. Even if the incentive for the English and French had been strategic, not aesthetic, it was impossible to ignore the beauty all around them. The scenery they'd been flashing through was spectacular, endless coconut and banana palms, glimpses of white sand and water, fluttering green against deep blue and silver. But she'd glimpsed poverty among the exclusive tourist enclaves. Women washed clothes in rivers. Men hacked at vegetation with ferocious-looking machetes. Tiny shacks appeared to be regular dwelling-places. They struck a stark contrast with the glistening hotels on the idyllic coves, where security gates appeared to mark a line between visitor and native.

And Marigot Bay undoubtedly fell into the former category, she reflected, sipping more orange juice and letting the zingy citrus sweetness slither cold and reviving down her throat. The sun was glittering remorselessly on rows of white yacht masts at the quayside. The lush, enclosing hills of the bay were dotted with vivid colour. Scarlet and orange flowers covered trees and palms. Guy Sterne's magnificent villa stood alone, on its own private crescent of beach. Long, low and sprawling, artistically draped with purple and cerise bougainvillaea, with terracotta pantiled roofs, and cool white walls. Inside it was cool and restful, with honey-coloured stone tiles covering a huge entrance hall, where she'd promptly dropped her suitcase and flight-bag and made a dive for the kitchen and the fridge to quench her raging thirst.

There'd been numerous dark arched carved-wood

doors leading off the hall, most of which she had still to investigate. . .

Hummingbird House. Guy Sterne's tropical hide-away. Easing the damp khaki cotton of her culotte suit away from her perspiring skin, she drained the glass of juice and dragged herself away from the mesmerising sight of the turquoise water and army of waving coconut palms. It might not be bedtime by St Lucian standards, but second on her list of essentials, after the long cold drink, was a cool shower, and a long, long lie down. But, in spite of her exhaustion, her senses were intrigued by her surroundings. There was something strangely pru-rient about a total freedom to examine someone else's personal tastes, but all her artistic antennae were quiv-ering as she moved back inside and began to look carefully around her.

A swift tour of inspection revealed numerous bed-rooms, an enormous sitting-room with a raised dining-area visible through an archway, and a whole wall of french doors opening on to an oval glittering blue swimming-pool. The Caribbean lapped on to the deserted palm-fringed beach just beyond.

Had Guy Sterne chosen furnishings and textiles for this villa himself? A faint tug of reluctant approval accompanied her investigations into colours and pat-terns. Whoever was responsible for the interior decora-tion of Hummingbird House had subtly co-ordinated paler, more restful shades of sun-gold and sea-blue. The result was a glorious panoply of sensual colour ranging from vibrant cobalt to cool mauve-blue, from sunflower yellow to melon. Yards of straw-coloured raw silk adorned the windows.

She studied the books in the bookcase, a mixture of

classics like Tolstoy and Trollope, Fitzgerald and Henry
James. There was even some Sartre, and Camus, and
then a large number of sailing books, books on art,
music, ballet. She gave up trying to analyse Guy Sterne's
character on the basis of his bookshelves. It was too
confusing.

She ran her fingers slowly over the stubbly, woven
texture of a wall-hanging, part woven, part collage. It
had a rough, rustic charm, earthy colours. Cane and
rattan furniture, beautiful paintings with the bold air of
Van Gogh or Gauguin. Strange carvings, in smooth
honey-coloured wood with themes of fruit and leaves,
with an African air about them. Had the notorious City
financier personally collected these examples of ethnic
art? It was possible, she conceded, that Guy Sterne
didn't spend twenty-four hours a day, three hundred
and sixty-five days a year ruthlessly tearing apart other
people's livelihoods. Even asset-strippers had to relax
and pursue a few hobbies from time to time. . .

But while her designer's eye revelled in it all she
decided she was going to rattle around here in solitary
splendour. The villa must sleep ten at least. Charles and
Lucy certainly knew how to pick their friends, she
thought drily. The owner of Hummingbird House might
be a surprisingly artistic, cultured hedonist, but here
was a man, she decided, who liked the good things in life
and didn't care how he made the money to acquire
them. . .

That disposed of the absent, mysterious but undoubtedly deeply offensive Guy Sterne.

Making her way back to the bedrooms, she chose the
biggest one with panoramic views across the surf-lapped

bay. An en-suite bathroom possessed soft banana-coloured towels and creamy, thyme-scented soap, and a shower. She lathered herself languidly beneath the refreshing jets of water, letting the spray caress every hot, sticky part of her with a glorious wave of sensual awareness. She released her hair from its restraining band; it tumbled in heavy red-gold waves past her shoulder-blades, and she shampooed it with her favourite herbal shampoo. Finally, reluctantly, she emerged and wrapped herself in a towel, then found another for her hair, winding it turban-style.

There was a fan on the ceiling of the bedroom. Drawing the heavy, lattice-patterned curtains across the window, she let the damp towel slip to the tiled floor, and lay full length on the bed, the matching pale blue and melon lattice-print bedspread soft and welcoming beneath her.

With a huge, exhausted yawn, she stretched and then lay spread-eagled, flat on her back.

Later, she'd unpack, later she'd explore Marigot Bay, later she'd organise herself some supper, later she'd start feeling excited, privileged, ecstatically lucky to be here. . .later she'd do all kinds of things, but right now ten solid hours of travelling, the latter part in that bone-shaker of a van, had left her utterly spent. She had to cool off, she had to rest. . .

She awoke with a jerk some time later, and lay staring blankly around her, for a few seconds quite unable to get her bearings. Everywhere was in darkness. She could almost hear her brain scurrying about in confusion, computer-fashion, seeking familiar data to confirm location.

Then it came back to her, the villa, falling asleep. She stretched and propped herself up on an elbow, aware that something was not quite right. It was pitch dark everywhere, and the whirr of the ceiling fan seemed to fill the silent bedroom.

But she'd heard something else. Something else had woken her. She listened, still half drugged from sleep, straining her ears intently, a touch of uneasiness making her blood begin to pound like a deep sea-swell in her veins.

There was somebody moving around in the villa.

Before she'd had a chance to react, to jump off the bed and snatch the towel, seize some kind of weapon to defend herself from whoever it was prowling around, the bedroom door swung open and the light clicked on.

Frozen in shock for a few seconds, she recovered her wits sufficiently to let out an outraged scream, and to catapult into a kneeling position, grabbing the bedspread to cover herself. Clutching it protectively in front of her, she stared in dry-mouthed terror at a very tall, dark, athletic-looking man, clad in a lightweight beige suit, with the jacket off and slung carelessly over his shoulder, suspended on one negligent finger. Lazy-lidded grey eyes in a dark, chisel-chinned face were regarding her with an insulting trace of laughter somewhere in their depths.

'Well, well. Goldilocks, I presume?' The voice was a deep, flat drawl, husky, richly amused. A wave of hot colour swept over her as she wriggled to somehow attach the bedspread around her without letting it slip and giving this mocking character another full frontal. The towel had fallen off her hair, and the damp red-golden waves fell across her eyes in a tousled curtain. She hated to think of the sight she'd just presented, sprawling inelegantly, stark naked on the bed. . .

'I *beg* your pardon?' Her voice shook with fury.

'As in "look who's sleeping in *my* bed"?' He explained, slanting a quizzical eyebrow.

'*Your* bed?' Slowly, light was dawning. Virginia glared at the intruder in sick dismay. Her throat dried. '*You're* Guy Sterne?'

'The same.' He took a casual step towards her, and extended a mock-polite hand. Virginia clenched her fingers tighter round the bedcover, her heart hammering against her ribs in panic. 'And unless you're one of Charity LeVille's nubile masseuses over from Gros Islet. . .' he'd reached the bed, and to her horror slung his jacket over a nearby chair and sat down on the edge of the bed, far too close for comfort, continuing in the same bland tone, '. . .which from the pious clutching of bedclothes I somehow doubt, maybe you'd like to explain exactly who *you* are?'

CHAPTER TWO

IT WAS rare for Virginia to be lost for words. But a combination of embarrassment, shock, and some other nameless disturbing emotion caused her initial protest to come out as a soundless squeak.

'I'm Virginia Chester,' she managed at last, in the quietly intense tone which would doubtless have triggered a red alert among family and friends alike. 'And this may be your villa, and your bed, but if you had the *minutest* atom of good manners or breeding you'd get out of here right now and let me get some clothes on!'

Guy Sterne's dark face possessed some indefinably tough, worldly-wise quality which made it almost impossible to read. It was hard to tell what he might be thinking.

'Unfortunately I've managed to acquire neither,' he said finally, straightening to his daunting height and sending a trickle of fear down her spine by tugging at the buttons on his shirt, apparently with every intention of undressing right there in front of her.

'What are you *doing*?' she demanded in a low, shaky voice.

'I'm hot, sweaty, tired, and I'm going to take a shower,' was the careless retort. 'If you're planning on staying, I suggest you move your stuff to one of the other bedrooms.'

The shirt was shrugged off to reveal a rock-hard male chest, copiously roughened with whorls of dark hair,

26

and, as he caught her mesmerised expression, a suspicion of a grin tweaked the corners of a wide, well-shaped mouth, the top lip heavily indented, the bottom lip fuller. He might even be passably attractive, Virginia told herself furiously, if it weren't for the villainous growth of stubble on his jaw. And if he weren't such a *lout*!

He was unfastening the waist of his trousers now, having kicked shoes and socks under a chair, and in helpless fury she bent down to snatch the damp towel from the floor, wrenching it round herself and jumping down from the bed, glaring at him so ferociously that he suddenly burst out laughing.

'It's all right, I didn't peek,' he assured her with a wolfish grin. 'I didn't need to—I've already seen enough! Your virtue's quite safe, incidentally.' The trousers had followed the jacket on to the chair, leaving only a pair of grey and white striped boxer shorts, and in dumb amazement she clutched the towel around her and stared reluctantly at the most impressive male body she'd ever seen, well over six feet of muscle and sinew and matt-looking olive-tanned skin. 'I don't go for redheads.'

'If you take anything else off before I've got my suitcase out of this room, I'll ring the police!' she announced with an icy calm she was far from feeling.

'OK, OK, I give in.' He raised his hands in the air in mock surrender, backing away, grey eyes suddenly dancing with genuine enjoyment. 'With my criminal record that could be the finish of my career! Mind you, this does give me an unfair advantage. Having seen the full extent of your naked charms, fair play decrees I reveal my own.'

'You seem to have a rather inflated idea of your own attractions, Mr Sterne,' she muttered, scarlet-faced, kicking her suitcase towards the door, and reaching cautiously behind her for the latch. 'And you obviously find this situation very entertaining. But frankly I find it *bloody* embarrassing!'

She'd reached the safety of the passageway, and slammed the door violently closed in his face. Grabbing her case, she marched along the passage to find a bedroom as far away from Guy Sterne's as possible, and pushed inside it, shutting the door and leaning weakly back against it, suddenly aware of how much she was trembling.

Calm down, an inner voice cautioned, as she stalked across the room to sit exhaustedly on a striped upholstered stool by a mirrored dressing-table. Calm down, and stop behaving like a shocked medieval nun. Try and see the funny side. Because there had to be one. The objectionable Guy Sterne had already spotted it, and was no doubt doubled up with mirth under the shower at this very moment. . .

But, try as she might, she couldn't laugh. She was too furious. Somewhere along the line, someone had got their wires crossed, that much was clear. Either the loathsome Mr Sterne had flown out here deliberately to coincide with her lonely holiday, which seemed most unlikely, or else Charles and Lucy had somehow omitted to inform him that Virginia was coming in their place. In that case, it was logical to assume that Guy Sterne had decided at the last minute to avail himself of his unexpectedly empty villa for an impromptu break in the sun.

The latter was possible, she supposed. Charles had a

mountain of worries at present, with Lucy's pregnancy, and Chester's imminent crisis. . .never renowned for his brilliant memory, her brother was slightly prone to flapping under pressure.

So what on earth should she do? Brazen it out? Try to alter her flight and go home tomorrow? Seek alternative accommodation somewhere, via the local tourist board maybe? That sounded expensive, and limited spending money was really all she had at her disposal, but could she seriously spend even one night under the same roof as that. . .that arrogant. . .*libertine*?

Jumping up, she flung open her suitcase and rummaged for something to wear, standing up to step into brief white silk bikini-pants. Catching sight of herself in a full-length, cane-framed mirror on the wall, she paused, a sick feeling growing inside her, and she groaned. It was too humiliating. . .she stared at her reflection, the damp tangle of hair tumbling over her eyes and down her back, the too pale, too thin length of arms and legs, the full thrust of high, ochre-tipped breasts, balanced by the curving jut of her hips. . .she put her hands to her face, and felt the heat in her cheeks.

She wasn't sure which would have been worse—open, lustful leering, or the teasing mockery she'd just been subjected to. Both equally mortifying, she decided bitterly.

She quickly pulled on the silk briefs, following with matching silk bra, short green- and peach-flowered culotte-skirt and a sleeveless cropped T-shirt in a toning shade of leaf-green. The material of the culottes was one of her own hand screen-prints. There were peaches, and bunches of grapes, entwined with leaves of varying shades and textures. It had been one of her favourites, during her course at the college. It boosted her morale now, just to wear it. She slid her bare feet into plaited-leather sandals, and faced the mirror with a touch more confidence. There, she looked presentable. Almost. Apart from her hair.

She ran her fingers through it quickly. It was almost dry. Dropping her head, she tugged a brush vigorously through the rippling red-gold, and then tossed it all back in a wild wavy curtain. No point even trying to contain it demurely now. Tomorrow it would have calmed down, but after washing it acquired too much zip and body to tame. Tortoiseshell combs would have to suffice. She met her reflection with a stubbornly squared chin, mentally preparing for battle.

But what kind of battle? she wondered apprehensively, discovering an exit from this bedroom which led on to a terrace, with an archway framing a velvety night sky filled with bright silver stars. Resting her arms on the wooden balustrade, she stared into the darkness, distracted by its unexpected beauty.

'"Hung be the heavens with black",' murmured a deep, cynical voice behind her, making her jump idiotically. '"Yield day to night".'

Guy Sterne came to lean beside her, clad now in worn-looking white canvas bermudas and a baggy black T-shirt. It was too dark to see his expression, but Virginia had no doubt it would be the same mocking smile. Stiffening, she straightened up. His nearness was disturbingly unwelcome.

'I wouldn't have classed you as a Shakespeare fan,' she said quietly, edging her way surreptitiously a foot further along the balustrade. 'But if you're quoting bits of *Henry VI Part One*, I'd have thought "Unbidden guests are often welcomest when they are gone" very appropriate.'

A click of a lighter illuminated the dark face beside her. Cigar smoke blended with the exotic perfumes on the night air. There was a thoughtful silence.

'Now there's an interesting response,' he said musingly. He turned and leaned his hips on the terrace railing, gazing into her face with disconcerting intensity. 'Intelligent, but touchy and insecure. How's that for instant character analysis?'

'Interesting,' she countered in soft annoyance, 'but arrogant.'

He gave a low, abrupt laugh. 'All right, you win. Like all females, you're bristling for an apology. Fine.' He straightened up, then bowed slightly, 'I apologise for barging in and finding you gloriously undressed on my bed, and for ordering you out while I took a shower. Most ill-bred and ungentlemanly of me.'

She could feel the heat flooding back into her cheeks. The unhurried, drawling delivery of this 'apology' was almost more insulting than the original incident.

'Don't give it another thought,' she retorted stiffly.

'That could prove difficult.' He was softly laughing at her. 'You were a pretty unforgettable sight——'

'For heavens' sake!' she burst out, goaded past restraint. 'Will you just stop going on about it?'

'What an uptight young lady you are.'

'I am *not* uptight. . .'

'No?' There was a warning glitter of laughter in his eyes, and casually he dropped his cigar to the terrace and ground it out under his heel, then moved a fraction closer to her. 'You strike me as the kind of fierce little feminist who thinks men are beneath her contempt, rapists one and all.'

'I can't say I really care how I strike you, Mr Sterne. . .' She was trembling slightly now, and furious with herself, but somehow his height and his blatant masculinity were sending shivers of trepidation down her spine. 'And you needn't worry; I've no intention of staying here long enough for you to continue insulting me. I'm going to walk down to the hotel on the other side of the bay and see if they've got any rooms free——'

She made it halfway past him, but then his hand shot out to detain her.

'Hey. . .calm down.' The tone was fractionally less mocking. His fingers felt warm and strong on her bare arm. She shivered involuntarily. 'There's no need to storm off into the night. Let's just get this situation straight. . .you're Virginia Chester, little sister of Charles? Correct?'

'Correct.' Why on earth was her heart hammering as if she'd run a marathon? Just because the wretched man was holding her arm?

'And Charles forgot to tell me you were coming here in his place.'

'It looks like it. Look, I'm sorry. . .' she agreed stiffly, 'You obviously thought you'd grab a quick break in the sun, and now you've found your privacy invaded. I can see why you're irritated. If you don't mind my sleeping here tonight, I'll make other arrangements in the morning.'

'You don't have to do that. And I'm not irritated. I was just hot and dusty and. . .surprised.' The wide mouth twisted in self-mockery. 'And I've got a warped sense of humour. My friends are always complaining about it. . .'

'You have friends?' She stared meaningfully at the place where his fingers were circling her upper arm, and he made a wry face and released her.

'A few.' His grin was so disarming that she blinked slightly. 'If I promise to stop teasing you, will you come out for dinner with me?'

It was on the tip of her tongue to say she'd rather have dinner with a snake, but then she stopped. This situation had strong elements of farce, and it suddenly struck her as in danger of getting out of hand. She was mature enough to accept an olive branch, even if it was being handed out tongue in cheek. And then there was this obnoxious man's involvement with Chester's to think of. . .if she allowed her instincts full rein and indulged her true feelings at this stage mightn't she be jeopardising Charles's hopes of help for Chester's?

With a slight shrug, she turned away to inspect the starry night again.

'There's food in the fridge,' she managed at last. 'I'd only intended to fix myself a light snack and get an early night. I crashed out on the bed before I got the chance. So there's absolutely no need to feel you've got to invite me out with you!'

'When you get to know me better, Virginia, you'll know martyrdom isn't my style.'

No, she agreed to herself, retreating to her bedroom to fetch her shoulder-bag and a light white cotton jacket, it wouldn't be. Guy Sterne projected a personality in which self-interest most emphatically came first. But it was silly to go into a major sulk. And, quite apart from demonstrating maturity by dismissing the incident and behaving normally, if she could manage to be polite to this man there was just a chance she might discover some clues to his plans for her family's business. Surely, the fact that he was out here, calmly taking a holiday, might be an encouraging sign? The machinations of corporate sharks were a slightly hazy area in her experience. Did this mean Guy Sterne didn't consider the crisis at Chester's to be *that* big a crisis, after all?

An uneasy atmosphere prevailed as an open-top jeep was located in a garage, and the bumpy ride was negotiated down to the marina. Sitting with her own bare legs close to a hairy, powerful-looking brown thigh, her fastidious gaze drawn to the flex and contraction of muscles as gears were changed, wasn't precisely conducive to Virginia's peace of mind, for some infuriating reason. She was relieved when they abandoned the jeep for a brief ferry ride across the bay, and stepped ashore at a softly lit veranda restaurant among swaying coconut palms.

The setting was so romantically idyllic, with the distant jangle of yacht masts, soft calypso music, the rustle of breeze in the palms, that she thought of Mortimer again with a sick wave of anger. It wasn't that she wanted him to be here with her. Perish the very *thought*. She'd be quite happy never to set eyes on him again. But it was the thought of how things *should* have been between them. Theirs had been a friendship she'd trusted and valued. Everything had been shattered when he'd brought another dimension into the situation, tried to force something she didn't want, something she didn't think she could ever face again. . .

'That's a very tragic expression,' her companion commented drily. 'Surely the prospect of eating dinner with me can't be that soul-destroying?'

'Of course not,' she countered politely, meeting the smiling eyes of the hovering waiter with a touch more warmth in her face. 'Sorry, I was miles away.'

'What do you want to drink? Would you like to try one of the local rum-based cocktails?'

'Well. . .' A waiter threaded past them with a tray of delicious looking amber-coloured drinks, with ice and fruit on top.

'Bring us two of those,' Guy suggested with a flicker of a smile, 'while we choose what to eat. Right, Miss Chester, what do you like? Meat? Fish? Shellfish? Spiced food or plain?'

'I'll try anything once. . .but how expensive is this place?' In all the upset and confusion, it had only just occurred to her that, even if this was a self-imposed discipline, her funds were limited. The generous allowance paid automatically into her bank account from her father had always struck Virginia as a vaguely insulting signal of the helpless dependence of his female offspring, negating the possibility of her supporting herself. It was probably a trivial, silly hang-up, she acknowledged in calmer moments. And it wasn't as if she was ungrateful for the financial assistance through college. But somehow to use the money for extravagant luxuries was another matter. One day soon she intended to pay it all back, with interest. Until then, she accepted it as graciously as she could for necessities only, much to her father's irritation. . .

'I don't have all that much spending money for this holiday,' she explained, seeing a flicker of surprised cynicism in Guy Sterne's eyes, and flushing a little. Rich little Daddy's girl, without any money? she could almost hear him thinking. 'So I don't want to splurge it all on one meal!'

'Don't worry about that. How about the langoustine in lime butter? They do it well here. Have you been to St Lucia before?'

'No, but——'

'They have fruit and vegetables you have to taste to believe. Christophine, green figs, calaloo, dasheen, yam. . .'

She made a cool face. 'They sound exotic. Do they taste good?'

'Try them and see.'

Their drinks arrived, and she sipped the richly flavoured combination tentatively.

'Different,' she gave as a verdict, keen not to appear girlishly bowled over by all these unusual tastes, opting for the shrimp special with deep-fried vegetables, and eyeing Guy Sterne's dark face with calm determination. 'And incidentally, I always pay my way, whoever I'm with. Tonight will obviously be no exception.'

'We'll see.' He gave a non-committal shrug, and sipped his drink, ordering steak stuffed with crayfish, and then regarding her with a slightly disconcerting intensity across the candlelit table.

'So, you're Charles's little sister.' The speculative tone, and the use of the word 'little' made her bristle all over again.

'I am twenty-one,' she pointed out, as evenly as she could.

'And you work in the family business as well?'

'No. . . I have shares in Chester's. But I've just finished a degree course in London.'

'In what subject? Where?'

'Textile design. At the Central School of Art.'

'And what do you hope to do with that qualification?'

'Ultimately, I'd like to start my own interior design company. But what is this, twenty questions?' She laughed slightly, to disguise her annoyance.

'I'm interested in knowing more about you,' he said musingly, leaning back in his chair, the heavy-lidded grey gaze unsettling her to a degree she found hard to accept. 'After all, since the intimacy of our initial introduction, I already know quite a lot.'

'Such as?' The challenge proved unwise. The dart of laughter in the worldly grey eyes grew sharper again.

'Such as. . .well, at least I know you're an authentic redhead.' He grinned unrepentantly, watching her deep blush of embarrassment with apparent fascination.

Virginia seethed silently. It was impossible to be polite and distant with this man. He was just too. . .*rude*!

'Tell me something, Mr Sterne,' she enquired softly. 'How old are you?'

'I'm thirty-two.' He smiled again. '*Definitely* grown up.'

'Don't fool yourself!' she exclaimed, incensed. 'You're about as grown up as. . .as Just William, with all this leering, these smutty innuendoes, just because you happened to see me with no clothes on!'

In her anger, the words had come out slightly louder than intended. A couple on a nearby table turned curiously to stare at them, and Virginia took a desperate mouthful of the rum mixture, suddenly aware that its potency was cleverly disguised beneath a fruity overtone.

Guy Sterne was having great difficulty in controlling his amusement. She glared at him across the glass-shaded candlelight, feeling a rare impulse to inflict physical violence.

'It wasn't *seeing* you with no clothes on,' he explained patiently, at last, suppressing laughter. 'It was your reaction to being seen with no clothes on! You were so impressively. . .outraged.'

She took a deep breath and controlled her pounding pulse-rate.

'If you had the intelligence of a retarded flea, Mr Sterne, might it have occurred to you that I was *frightened*?' she queried sweetly. 'I was alone in a strange villa, and woke up to hear someone prowling round! I was hardly likely to sit up in bed and say "Do come in, have we met?" was I?'

He looked briefly down at his plate, which had just arrived bearing succulent-looking food and wafting a tempting aroma, then glanced up at her again. The grey gaze was still amused, but there was a suggestion less mockery there.

'I stand rebuked. I'm sorry if I frightened you,' he said softly, nodding to her plate. 'Your shrimps have arrived.'

The meal was mouth-watering. In another uneasy silence, they ate for a while, and when the wine-waiter brought a bottle of white Californian wine she felt too preoccupied to refuse when Guy poured some into her glass.

It seemed his turn, too, to appear lost in thought. She watched him covertly while he deftly impaled a wedge of fillet steak on his fork, and put it in his mouth. Actively disliking him, she nevertheless realised that she found his company annoyingly. . .disturbing? Was that the word? There was a strangely *compelling* quality about him. She felt confused by this private admission. She disliked the sensation of being unable to analyse what was going on, either in her own head or in his, which could possibly produce this. . .shiver of reaction? Mild jet lag, she told herself impatiently, spearing a prawn and biting into its juicy firmness. Her brain wasn't functioning correctly. Because the tension inside her had to be cerebral. It certainly couldn't be physical. She thought of Mortimer and shivered slightly. No, definitely not physical. . . She eyed, with as much dispassion as she could muster, the broad athlete's physique of the man opposite her across the white-clothed table. Flat-muscled, radiating cool, relaxed strength, admittedly he was an impressive sight. But he was hardly the first good-looking man she'd had dinner with.

As if to reassure herself, she coldly analysed his features from under thick gold-brown eyelashes. Dark, olive-tinged skin, with a hint of almost Mediterranean swarthiness. . .thick, dark hair, straight and standing up slightly at the front, swept back and cut short round the ears. . .a long, wide, 'boxer's' sort of nose. Thick dark eyebrows over those unnerving deepset eyes.

No, there wasn't any particular feature to account for it, she decided irritably. He was just one of those people whose presence projected authority, perhaps. Was there maybe a sneaking feeling that, if he wasn't laughing at her, he was usually laughing at life in general, and that he might be quite fun to be with?

She dismissed the conjecture instantly. Guy Sterne would be about as much fun to be with as one of the barracuda swimming in the coral reefs around the island. Vicious and unpredictable.

He looked up suddenly, and caught her staring at him. Transfixed for a second, she was trapped in the glitter of his eyes. They were extraordinarily pale. There was a hint of green in the grey. She swallowed quickly, and wrenched her eyes away.

'How long have you known my brother?' she asked politely, feeling driven to make some effort at conversation.

'Charles and I were at Sussex together. We've kept in touch through sailing.'

'Oh. Where do you sail?'

'I've got a ketch moored on the Hamble. I do some racing.'

Virginia nodded slowly. Lucy frequently mentioned Charles's sailing weekends. So that was where he disappeared to.

'Why? Do you sail?'

'What? Oh, no, not really. . . I. . .just wondered why Charles picked on you as. . .as. . .'

Guy Sterne was eyeing her with amused curiosity. Furious, she glared at her half-empty wine glass, realising that in her abstracted mood she'd drunk far more than she normally allowed herself to drink. The dull ache in her temples heralded another dismal headache, and here she was blurting out her thoughts without due care and attention.

'Go on,' he prompted softly, as she bit her lip. 'What has Charles picked me as?'

It was too late now. And, on reflection, she might as well come straight to the point. That was the only reason she was having dinner with this foul man, wasn't it?'

'As a potential saviour of Chester's?' she queried lightly, seeing a dark gleam come into his eyes.

'Who said Charles picked on me? How do you know it wasn't the other way around?'

'Well, from what was said at the board meeting. . .'

'And forget the "potential saviour" description,' Guy added, finishing his meal and taking a sip of wine. 'I'm no philanthropist, Miss Chester.'

No, I'll bet you're not, she thought in silent anger. But there *was* an element of doing a favour for a friend, she thought warily. From what Charles had said, he was pinning his hopes on Guy, for some reason, even though she sensed her brother's uneasiness. Guy Sterne must presumably have been a last-ditch contact. Desperate needs, and all that. . .but wasn't Charles playing the guileless chicken to Guy Sterne's wily fox?

'Naturally you're no philanthropist. But all Chester's needs is some healthy investment, plus a new line to augment the present systems——'

'I suspect what Sarah Chester Fabrics needs is a very large kick up the management's backside, and some fairly hefty streamlining of its present systems, before anyone will even contemplate healthy investment, Miss Chester.'

'That's not true!' She felt rising anger at the negligent way he was dismissing the company. 'I'm sure when you bother to go and see for yourself you'll find Chester's a very attractive investment proposition!'

'Is that so, Miss Chester?'

'Yes, it is! And for heaven's sake stop calling me Miss Chester. You make me sound like a Victorian governess!'

'OK, you're Virginia. I'm Guy. I have to admit it sounds a lot cosier if we're due to spend the next few nights under the same roof.'

'We're not! I'll make arrangements to move out tomorrow——'

'Unnecessary. Do you want any pudding?'

'No, thank you.' Her head was pounding now, a result

of the tension of the evening, she suspected, and the
near-homicidal tendencies she was discovering in the
company of this thoroughly unpleasant man. Plus the
wine she'd drunk. She wasn't used to drinking alcohol,
since she'd been ill.

'Coffee?'

'No. Thank you. But you go ahead. . .' She closed her
eyes for a second, and then opened them to see a glimpse
of concern on Guy Sterne's dark face.

'Are you all right?'

'Yes, I'm fine. At least. . .' She hesitated, suddenly
desperate to escape, to find somewhere quiet and dark
to lie down. 'I'm sorry, I'm afraid I'm not feeling quite
right. . .'

The dizzy feeling in her head intensified, and with an
abrupt surge of panic she knew she was about to black
out. She grasped the table, trying to stand up, slipped
and grabbed wildly at the cloth, sending plates, glasses,
wine bottle, crashing to the ground, and then with an
inner groan of dismay she watched the stone terrace rush
abruptly towards her face before everything went dark.

CHAPTER THREE

'It's OK. You're all right. You're quite safe. . .' The deep, concerned voice broke through the dark haze of unconsciousness, and she blinked and stared up at the shadowy image of Guy Sterne's face, bending over her.

'Oh, hell. . .' she groaned, and tried to sit up, her head feeling as if someone had stuffed it full of cotton wool, 'I fainted, didn't I? Oh, damn and *blast*. . .'

The dark face was a study in rueful amusement as he helped her to her feet to face the worried circle of fellow-diners and waiters hovering to offer assistance.

'It's no good "effing and blinding",' he remonstrated mildly, holding her firmly by the shoulders and inspecting her with a brilliantly dispassionate gaze. 'That won't cure fainting fits. What's your problem? Secret pregnancy? Anorexia nervosa?' He ran firm, warm hands over the slender elongated length of her upper arms as he spoke, adding softly, 'You're thin enough, that's for sure.'

Anger was a luxury she lacked the energy for, right that minute. Besides, she told herself, this man's rudeness didn't merit any response.

'Just take me back to the villa, please?' she managed to request, precariously clinging to her dignity.

With surprising gallantry, Guy Sterne complied. The bill was rapidly settled, and the brief journey back to the jeep completed in record time, with a firm supporting arm round her waist sending shivers of awareness through her.

The pot-holed drive back up to Hummingbird House did nothing to improve her state of health. She just made it to the bathroom in time, before she parted unceremoniously with the contents of her stomach, then hung weakly against the side of the washbasin, more wretched and humiliated than she'd ever felt in her life.

Finally, ashen-faced, she emerged to find Guy Sterne lounging patiently in the corridor outside. Thank God he hadn't barged into the bathroom to ministrate. But that was hardly surprising. He might radiate power and control but he didn't strike her as the kind of man who would number nursing skills among his repertoire.

'I think you should get into bed. I'll ring the doctor,' he said calmly.

'I. . .there's no need for a doctor. . .'

'No?' The cocked eyebrow indicated that he was re-examining his previous cynical stabs at her ailment.

'No! I know precisely what's wrong with me. . .'

'Good. Get into bed, I'll bring you some water, and you can tell me all about it.'

He turned on his heel and disappeared. Hesitating a moment, Virginia suddenly saw little point in arguing. Bed was where she most longed to be. While he went in search of the water, she locked herself furiously in the bathroom to don a baggy navy and white striped T-shirt nightdress, and by the time he returned she was safely hidden underneath the printed white bedspread. This room was decorated in a variety of vivid greens, blues and yellows. The white cotton bedspread had a simple, exotic print of palm trees, parrots and huge golden suns.

In more relaxed circumstances, its boldness and simplicity would no doubt have appealed strongly to her creative senses.

'Right.' The glass of water was placed at her bedside, and Guy Sterne sat on the side of the bed, far too close for her peace of mind. 'How are you feeling now?'

'I just have a headache. Once I take a couple of painkillers, I'll be fine.'

She met the searching gaze, as she swallowed two headache tablets.

'I am not pregnant, nor do I suffer from anorexia,' she added frostily, 'I'm trying to shake off an illness I've had for a few months, that's all.'

'What illness?' The penetrating grey eyes had narrowed thoughtfully on her pale face.

'Not that it's any of your damn business, but I've had glandular fever.'

'Ah.' Guy Sterne nodded slowly, 'Fever, headaches, fatigue, depression. The dreaded EB virus.'

'The what?' She drank some more water, glaring at him in fresh annoyance.

'Epstein and Barr, two physicians who identified the virus.'

'How on earth do you know so much about it? Have you had it as well?'

'Nope. My father's a doctor.' He spoke abruptly, as if the subject of his father was one he generally tried to avoid. Virginia stared at him in sudden curiosity. There was a flicker of something else in the shadowy gaze now. A shade less mockery. A suggestion of suppressed bitterness.

'Well, I'm over it now, I'm nearly better,' she began coolly, then saw his disbelief. 'I hardly *ever* black out, if that's what you're thinking! It's just been a long, exhausting day——'

'Sorry. I should have left you to fix your light snack and have an early night. The journey out here can be pretty tiring. You flew to Hewanorra?'

'Didn't you?'

He shook his head slightly, his expression detached. 'I stopped over in Barbados. Caught a local flight across to Vigie. It's just a short hop here by taxi.'

'Bully for you,' she muttered acidly. 'I had a couple of hours in a bone-shaker of a fur-lined mini-van!'

'Noble Soloman's?' The dark face creased in sudden laughter. 'He's very proud of that taxi service. Don't ever let him hear you describe his mini-van as a bone-shaker!'

'He was very sweet,' she conceded, her eyelids drooping exhaustedly despite her tension in this man's unwelcome presence, 'And I certainly wouldn't dream of insulting his mode of transport. Look, if the interrogation is over for tonight, do you mind if I go to sleep?' Suddenly it was as if she'd been drugged. The waves of tiredness were overpowering.

'If there's nothing else I can get you?' He straightened up easily as he spoke, and the lidded gaze moved laconically down over the outline of her body beneath the thin bedcover. Even in her weary state, she couldn't stop herself from wriggling self-consciously. For an agonising moment it felt as if she was naked again, under the intent, laughing scrutiny of those cruel grey eyes. To her intense horror, her nipples peaked and hardened under his gaze, without volition. Biting her full lower lip hard between her teeth, she crossed her arms quickly over her

breasts, but not before the glimmer of recognition in
Guy Sterne's enigmatic eyes.

'Goodnight. Sweet dreams,' he murmured drily, stroll-
ing to the door.

She couldn't bring herself to reply.

Face flaming, she clicked off the Tiffany bedside lamp,
slid down beneath the sheet and lay trembling with
surprise and self-disgust in the darkness as the door
closed behind him. It just wasn't possible. After the
fiasco with Mortimer it just wasn't possible that
this. . .this *insulting* individual could arouse even the
slightest flicker of response in her, was it?

With the question circling around in her head, and
certain she would lie awake in confused alarm, she fell
asleep almost instantly.

Her first thought in the morning was that she'd failed to
pay her share of the meal last night. In all the confusion
Guy Sterne had calmly flashed a credit card and whisked
her away. She should be grateful for that, at least. But
she'd have to find some way of squaring the situation.

Another thought struck her, as she showered and
peered blearily out of the windows at the translucent
blue and gold morning on the horizon. She'd promised
to ring Dad, Charles and Lucy when she arrived, to
reassure them of her safety. Guilt gnawed at her as she
pulled on a high-cut navy and white striped swimsuit,
with a printed fuchsia flower breaking the uniform stripe
over her left hip. They might be worrying themselves
sick, thinking she'd had an accident. Knotting on the
matching pareo, she made a mental note to telephone
them as soon as she collected her wits enough to work
out the time in the UK. With her erstwhile host's kind

permission, she reminded herself bitterly. Her stomach plummeted at the thought of meeting the sardonic Guy Sterne again this morning. Particularly in the enforced intimacy of the breakfast ritual.

At least her headache had gone, she reflected, securing her hair in a mass of Titian curls at her nape with a blue banana clip, and surveying the shadowed pallor of her face with grim resignation. The set-back of last night's fainting fit had shaken her. Low blood-pressure had been an unexpected side-effect of the glandular fever, but she'd been sure she'd come through all that. Blacking out at the restaurant had dashed those hopes.

She carefully packed her case again, then scanned the tidy bedroom and bathroom with some satisfaction. You could scarcely see anyone had been there. The sooner she was long gone the better. A walk down to the hotels on the other side of the bay should supply some clues on alternative accommodation. The island couldn't be bursting at the seams, surely? The money in her bank account was going to be put to good use, on this occasion. This was an emergency.

Barefoot, she tracked through the tiled hall, through the enormous sitting-room, towards the open french doors. The wind was billowing the silk curtains on its way through the acres of banana palms. The sunlight outside was dazzling, despite a bank of ominous dark clouds on the horizon.

Guy Sterne's sun-bronzed form was visible on a sun-lounger by the azure swimming-pool, impressive in Raybans and brief black swimming-trunks. A white ceramic coffee-pot and cups stood on a tray on a nearby table. A newspaper was spread out on the tiled pool

surround, and he was murmuring laconically into a
cordless telephone.

Probably on a hot-line to the world stock exchanges,
she thought crossly. The archetypal yuppie relaxing in
his island hideaway.

'Good morning.' The greeting was calm. He lifted one
sinewy arm to wave. As she walked slowly in his
direction, a tall girl with long, wavy black hair came
gracefully out of the door which led into the kitchen.
Virginia almost collided with her, and received a warm
but slightly wary smile in return. With confused feelings,
she smiled back, but she found herself staring in what
she realised must seem a naïve display of stunned
surprise.

In a minuscule black and white bikini, the girl was
extraordinarily beautiful. Sleek, long-limbed, with
smooth, velvety-looking skin the colour of bleached
coffee beans. She had the softest charcoal-brown eyes
Virginia had ever seen. Instantly, despite being blessed
with a slender-limbed, curvy figure herself, and skin
which bore no sign of the freckles often associated with
red hair, Virginia felt unprepossessing, blotchy, boring
and depressingly unfeminine in comparison. Unbidden,
last night's insults came creeping back.

So this was Guy Sterne's type of woman, an irritating
little voice niggled the back of her mind. No wonder he
didn't 'go for redheads', as he'd so crudely put it. Once
a man had seen this type of dusky-skinned beauty, she
imagined nothing else would do. Would the girl be
described as half-caste? What did it matter? She was
breathtakingly lovely. Virginia brushed the *frisson* of
pique aside. She couldn't care less what type of woman
Guy Sterne went for.

'Hi. I'm Tara.' The girl was holding out a small, delicate-looking hand, eyeing her with polite curiosity.

'Virginia Chester. How do you do?'

Her own capable, long-fingered hand seemed to dwarf the other girl's as they shook hands in greeting, and Virginia inwardly winced again. She wasn't sure her currently fragile ego could withstand much of Tara.

'Would you like me to get you some breakfast? There's fruit, rolls, coffee. . .' The soft voice was easy on the ear, the Caribbean vowels lazily drawn-out.

'That's all right, thanks. I can help myself to something. . .' She walked past Tara to where Guy Sterne still lounged on his chair, keeping her eyes level as she met his. The look she encountered was difficult to read.

'Good morning. Sorry about the scene at the restaurant. I felt an idiot, blacking out like that. You must tell me what I owe you for the meal. May I use your telephone? I promised I'd ring home as soon as I arrived yesterday, but somehow. . .with all the mix-up. . .I forgot. . .'

She was gabbling nervously, she realised, gradually petering to a halt as the implacable dark face didn't register any reaction whatsoever. It was the dark Raybans that made it impossible to tell what he was thinking. Then, finally, the wide, well-shaped mouth curved into a slightly smug smile.

'Forget about last night. That includes the price of the meal. And don't worry. I've spoken to Charles and your father. They know you're safe. I've promised to keep an eye on you.'

He reached over to weigh the coffee-pot in his hand, and gestured to Tara, who came quickly across.

'Fetch Miss Chester some hot coffee, and some warm rolls, will you, Tara?'

'Sure.' With a calm smile, the girl swung the empty pot into her hand and swayed with lazy sensuality towards the kitchen. All Virginia's feminist sympathies screamed outrage at the casual order to wait on her. If she'd had any doubts about Tara's relationship with the villa's owner, they rapidly evaporated as she watched the other girl's body language in graceful retreat. Guy Sterne was just the kind of man to treat women as objects for sexual gratification, and as obliging servants to keep house and serve his meals. . .

Tense with resentment, Virginia rounded on the inert man by the pool.

'I'd rather have spoken to my family personally. And what on earth do you mean, you've "promised to keep an eye on me"?'

What seemed a daunting quantity of hard male muscle clenched into action as he sat up and swung his long legs to the ground. Elbows on his knees, he took off the sunglasses and fixed the mocking grey gaze on her.

'Exactly that,' he said after a long pause. 'Your father was worried about your blackout last night. . .'

'You told him about that?' She was almost speechless with anger now. Hands on hips, aqua-green eyes darkening with emotion, she glared at him in defiant disbelief, 'You had no right to worry my father like that! He didn't know about any of my fainting fits——'

'How many have there been?'

'Only three, including last night, but——'

'That's three too many. I gathered none of your family knew about it. Are you normally so secretive?'

She took a long, deep breath to control herself.

'Secrecy has nothing to do with it. I was away at college. I didn't want them fussing, trying to persuade me to give up and come home. . .!' She glared at Guy Sterne's motionless, strangely immobile expression in helpless fury. Quite apart from her reluctance to give her family any more ammunition to treat her like a witless child, Guy Sterne's arrogant interference had merely burdened Charles and her father with yet another worry to add to their depressing catalogue of troubles. She felt like strangling him.

'You had no right to tell them,' she began in a low, fiery voice. 'Charles is worried about Lucy's pregnancy, and Dad's worried sick over the business. . .' She stopped, aware that her tongue was running away with her in the heat of the moment. The unnerving grey-green eyes narrowed slightly, and as Tara appeared with a tray he gestured for Virginia to sit at the table, his gaze not leaving her as she reluctantly did so.

'I can see why they were so keen for you to take a holiday,' he said thoughtfully, eyeing the rigid line of her shoulders above the scoop neck of her swimsuit. 'You're too tense. A few days here in Marigot Bay should sort you out.' He grinned suddenly, disarmingly, mimicking the long, sun-drenched vowel-sounds of the St Lucians, 'Hang loose, stay cool, baby!'

'Very amusing,' she retorted stiffly. 'But I don't intend staying here in Marigot Bay much past breakfast-time. I'll take a taxi into the nearest town and seek alternative accommodation.' She spread butter on to a deliciously aromatic roll, and spread it with honey, adding calmly, 'This is your villa. You've every right to be here. I shan't impose any longer than I can help.'

'You're not going anywhere.' The words were so softly

spoken that she wondered at first if she'd heard correctly. He'd stood up as he spoke, and came to loom disturbingly large over her before spinning one of the chairs at the table and straddling it, resting his forearms on the back and fixing her with an unfathomable gaze.

'I beg your pardon?' she began coldly, but he interrupted her.

'What are you frightened of?' The deep voice was quietly probing, slightly mocking. 'Me?'

'Don't be so absurd!' she snapped, reddening. 'Why on earth should I be frightened of you?' She glanced round as she spoke, wondering if the beautiful Tara was nearby, enjoying the curious argument. The dark girl had dived into the bright turquoise swimming-pool, and was swimming up and down in a leisurely breast-stroke, moving through the myriad white marble reflections in the water like a fish. She twisted her gaze back to the man opposite her.

'Search me why you should be.' He shrugged magnificent pectorals, and smiled a rather lop-sided grin. 'My last aggravated rape charge was at least twelve months ago. I'm considered a reformed character these days.'

'For heaven's sake! Do you bring *everything* down to the level of sexual innuendo?'

'I do my best.' He leaned over to the tray, picking up the coffee-pot. 'How do you like your coffee?'

'Weak and white, no sugar,' she snapped, forgetting her manners completely in her intense dislike of the man sitting far too close for comfort.

'That figures.' He poured equal quantities of coffee and hot milk into a cup and handed it to her with a mocking grin.

'I suppose you like yours strong and black?' she enquired with saccharine civility.

'Almost right. Black with a dash.' He poured himself a fresh cup, and eyed her with a level scrutiny. 'Now, let's get a few things straight. I didn't ring your family with the sole intention of provoking another of your temper tantrums, however entertaining I may find them. I needed to tell Charles where I was. I flew out here on impulse. With Sarah Chester's on the brink of insolvency it occurred to me he might be panicking. . .'

Virginia felt a cold shiver down her spine.

'My brother Charles seemed to naïvely imagine you were just the person to put everything right,' she said, picking her words carefully, trying to control the fury chilling her inside. 'He was calling you in as the ultimate specialist. So tell me, if the business my grandmother started several decades ago really *is* on the brink of insolvency, how come you're sunning yourself in the Caribbean, Mr Sterne? You don't look to me like someone desperately struggling to nurse a company-patient back to life. You look like someone who's waiting for the patient to die. So you can carve up the remains and sell them off to the highest bidders?'

He took a sip of coffee and leant back, eyeing her intently.

Something in the pale gaze was so unnerving that she froze. The teasing light had abruptly switched off. So that was where the insufferable Mr Sterne was vulnerable, she found herself noting abstractedly. He didn't like people nit-picking about his ruthless financial tactics.

'For a twenty-one-year-old, you've a depressingly cynical outlook, Virginia.' The deep drawl had become very quiet, so that it was impossible to tell if he was angry or just bored.

'I'm not a cynic, I'm a realist! It's people like you who are the cynics——'

'And who are "people like me"?' he queried mildly.

'People who always have an eye for the main chance! Who see everything in terms of. . .of balance sheets and profitability and viability!' Anger and frustration made her warm to her theme regardless of diplomacy. 'I'm no cynic, I care about the people who work for Sarah Chester's, I care about the ideals my grandparents believed in, about the welfare of the employees, their physical and mental well-being, their degree of satisfaction in creating something that's positively useful and worthwhile in this world. . .'

'What a passionate speech,' he drawled laconically, reaching for the Raybans and sliding them over heavy-lidded eyes. 'Very commendable. But your brand of realism seems to be tinged with ideology. Unfortunately ideology doesn't create jobs, Virginia.'

'Yes, but profit isn't everything——'

'On the contrary, in the *real* business world profit is the key to expansion. And expansion is the only way to keep the shareholders happy.'

Guy Sterne leaned forward to drink some more coffee, his wide mouth suddenly twisting humorously.

'At least Sarah Chester Fabrics is one thing we have in common to while away the lazy Caribbean evenings, Miss Chester, whichever side of the fence we're on.'

'I can't possibly stay here.'

'Why not? Hummingbird House sleeps eight. All the bedrooms have their own en-suite bathrooms. If it's a chaperon you're after, Tara lives in whenever I come here. So why not relax and enjoy yourself? Why go storming off wasting money on another place to stay?'

A dark eyebrow cocked enquiringly. Virginia stared down at the half-eaten roll on her plate, and took a shaky sip of coffee. After her outburst, she was already regretting her lack of control. Damn her hot temper. It wouldn't help the company, insulting the man called in to help them. . .this infuriating situation could even prove a godsend to Chester's, if she could manage to suppress her emotions and be objective about things, couldn't it? It was even possible that she could argue the case for Chester's survival in a calm, rational way, if only she could overcome this personal aversion to her unwelcome holiday companion!

She shivered slightly, despite the sun.

'In your state of health, I'd say the less stress, the better,' he added, softly patient. 'Your brother says you've been pushing yourself too hard, trying to finish your degree when you should have been resting.'

'I'm glad you've had such a cosy chat about me!'

'Lucy said she'd ring you this evening. Give you time to sleep off your jet lag.'

'Did she?' She drank some more coffee, feeling decidedly manipulated. If she marched out, it was going to turn into a major incident. She'd never hear the end of it when she got home.

Her brain seemed to be arguing with itself. She blinked, focusing on the unbelievably white crescent of sand framed by waving coconut palms beyond the pool. What was the big deal? she demanded silently. She could contain her dislike for this character for a few days, couldn't she? And as for last night's embarrassment, hurt pride could heal, if she set her mind to it. It hadn't

actually been Guy Sterne's *fault* that he'd barged in and
found her naked in his bedroom last night, even if his
mocking treatment of the incident had been grossly
insulting. . .

'All right,' she said quietly, 'if you really don't mind
my playing gooseberry. . .'

'Playing gooseberry?' For a moment, the grey eyes
were blank. Then he gave a sudden short bark of
laughter. 'Fine. I don't mind you playing gooseberry at
all.'

Did she imagine a faint degree of tension suddenly
evaporating from Guy Sterne's cool, enigmatic
expression? 'You won't regret it.'

She managed a cautiously cool smile. 'Really?'

'You've just landed yourself the best guide on the
island, Miss Chester. You did say you enjoyed sailing?'

'I. . .' She went blank. Had she said that? 'I don't
dislike it, but I've only been out with Charles about three
times. . .'

'Road travel can be a touch bumpy.' He grinned
suddenly, and she recalled her trip from the airport and
for once agreed wholeheartedly with Guy Sterne. 'I've
got a neat little ketch moored down at the marina.
Useful for getting around.'

'Look. . .' she began in a cool voice, glancing round
for Tara, who seemed to have disappeared into the
house, 'when I used the phrase "playing gooseberry", I
was referring to my staying at Hummingbird House. I
certainly wouldn't dream of tagging along with you and
Tara when you go sailing or sightseeing or whatever. . .'

'Tara's seen it all,' he pointed out softly. 'She lives
here.'

'Yes, but even so——'

'First stop,' he went on, as if she hadn't spoken, 'Soufrière. The mineral baths. They're supposed to cure all sorts of things from poor nerves to hangovers. Just the thing for a twitching little nervous wreck who keeps passing out on her dinner dates. We'll leave in an hour. All right with you?'

'Well, I really don't——'

'Bring a towel.'

Without waiting for her answer, Guy Sterne straightened up, strolled to the edge of the pool, and dived effortlessly into the turquoise water. With a churning, helpless feeling inside, Virginia watched the dark body slicing down the length of the pool in a faultless front crawl.

He was an impressive sight. She watched him for as long as she could bear to, anger warring with a sense of duty, then abruptly she marched into the house, and with gritted teeth and a distinctly martyred feeling she began to resentfully sort out a bag to take with her to Soufrière.

CHAPTER FOUR

'So WHAT do you think of the *Buccaneer*?'

Guy Sterne glanced over from his nonchalant position at the tiller. 'Like it?'

Virginia returned his look through half-closed eyes, behind the protective anonymity of her sunglasses. She was feeling helpless, a victim of circumstances temporarily outside her control, and it was a feeling she loathed.

She was supposed to be relaxing, she reflected wryly. And surely relaxing should be the easiest thing in the world, lazing in the jewel-like brilliance of the Caribbean waters, with the trade winds blowing them steadily southwards.

But how could she relax in the company of a man she didn't like, didn't trust, and who alternately mocked, patronised and bullied? Even more disturbing, though she shrank from admitting it, was this subtle sexual threat. It lurked tormentingly just below the surface. And it alarmed her, to say the least. She liked to be in control, and this feeling gave the impression it could get out of control. . .

She thrust her hands into her pockets, and gritted her teeth. This was crazy. She must be imagining it. There was no way Guy Sterne could be remotely interested in *her*, and as for the other way around. . .

She shivered. After what happened with Mortimer, she'd voted herself off men for life. And as for *this*

59

particular man? She'd rather throw herself to the lions. . .

'Yes. I like it. . .' She dropped her head back to relieve the tension in her neck, and gazed up at the rigging. The snowy white mainsail was stretched on a taut close-hauled setting in the wind. Her gaze moved slowly over the dazzling white decks, and into the dark well of the cabin.

'And I must admit I'm enjoying this.' She forced a cool, sociable air, determined to make the effort at normal, light conversation to disguise this mounting unease inside her. 'I can't claim to be a sailing fanatic, but this is a lot more civilised than battling through a Force Six in the Solent, togged up like an alien from outer space in thermals and foul-weather gear!'

'A fair-weather sailor.'

'I'm afraid so.'

'Nothing wrong with that. If you drive yourself fairly hard in most areas of your life, it doesn't hurt to take the easy option in your leisure time.'

He eased himself out of his wedged position in the cockpit and beckoned her over. 'Take the helm for a while. I'll go below and fix us a drink.'

She'd swapped the pareo for white bermudas and a loose navy and white striped T-shirt to keep the scorching sun off her shoulders. Passing him in the cramped area of the cockpit, her bare leg brushed against the coarseness of his knee. She flinched away as if she'd been burnt. He scanned her tense expression, his eyes crinkled up against the sun. It was hard to see if he was amused, or just squinting into the glare.

'Hey, relax,' he advised softly, putting the tiller between her nerveless fingers and flicking her lightly under the chin. 'Your nerves are shot, Miss Chester. You're a prime candidate for the laid-back Caribbean lifestyle.'

'I'm perfectly all right,' she snapped abruptly, feeling the ketch respond to her tug on the rudder. The sensation of being in control of the boat, at least, was oddly comforting. 'Did you say something about a drink?'

'Yes, ma'am.' He touched his forehead in mock humility, and ducked down below. 'At your service, ma'am.'

She ignored him, one eye on the distant coastline, the other on the automatic compass.

'She's a neat little boat,' she commented coolly, accepting a long glass of orange juice and fizzy mineral water. 'Though I'm surprised you haven't got something on a grander scale.'

His eyes were hidden behind the Raybans again now, but his sideways glance was quizzical. 'I like sailing single-handed. Anything bigger than this is too much like hard work.'

'Really?'

The wry hint of sarcasm in her voice hung in the silence.

'Tell me,' he said at last, conversationally, stretching out along the cockpit seat and crossing long hard legs at the ankles in front of him, 'is blatant prejudice a temporary flaw, or a permanent feature of your personality?'

She looked round at him abruptly. The dark face was devoid of expression.

'I'm not prejudiced. . .'

'I was thinking about your outburst earlier on, by the pool. You make sweeping judgements, Virginia. Without hard evidence. You've assigned me the role of heartless villain financier, obsessed with money, wealth, and luxury. Were you expecting the royal yacht *Britannia*, complete with resident crew?'

For a few moments, she was speechless. This was so nearly true that she had the grace to feel slightly ashamed of herself. Hastily she rallied her defences.

'Maybe Schreider Sterne Inc. needs to get a reputation for giving away half its profits to charity before I change my perceptions about your lifestyle!'

'So you've made a study of my lifestyle? Should I be flattered?' He sounded infuriatingly unmoved.

'Your name appears quite regularly in the financial pages. And a friend at college had an uncle whose company was taken over by Schreider Sterne. It doesn't take a doctorate in high finance to notice when a group of companies regularly gobbles up other companies, regardless of their line of business, efficiently dismantles them, and sells off any bits worth selling off, at a healthy profit!'

'I imagine art school is a place where you sit up all hours putting the world to rights?'

'Don't be so. . .patronising,' she countered in a low, angry voice. 'At least art schools teach students how to produce something worthwhile, something. . .*tangible*, during their lives! What have *you* ever produced that. . .that could *benefit* the quality of anyone else's life?'

There was a short pause.

'You have to admit I mix a mean orange-juice spritzer.'

She flashed him a withering look, and saw the mocking tilt of his mouth.

'I dare say that sums up the extent of your humanitarian ambitions!' she snapped shortly, then with an inward groan she belatedly remembered her worthy intentions regarding Sarah Chester's. She could have bitten off her impulsive tongue. Fat chance she had of influencing Guy Sterne's decisions over the fate of the family firm if every time she entered into conversation with him she ended up insulting him. Even if the insults were skilfully repaid with interest.

He was watching her inner battle with casual amusement. Could he read her mind? she wondered angrily. Did he know exactly the kind of dilemma she found herself in? If he did, he was in an enviable position to play cat and mouse with her for the duration of their stay. It was a case of either meekly playing along and being polite, or blowing all her chances in constant conflict with the wretched man. . .

'I'll tell you what,' he suggested softly, as if he might be making it easy for her, although she couldn't imagine why he should. 'In the interests of your convalescence, let's call a truce.'

'A truce?' She was even more uneasy now. That dark, purring kind of voice he was using sent chills down her back.

'You know, cessation of hostilities? You stop firing at me, and I stop sniping back? Then I can relax and enjoy my holiday, and you can direct all that pent-up aggression to killing off your virus?'

It was on the tip of her tongue to tell him to keep his supercilious consideration to himself. But on reflection what he said sounded perfectly reasonable, despite the ever-present note of wry mockery. Why on earth was it such an enormous effort to force a bland expression, and shrug and nod?

'OK, fine by me. It's too hot to bicker.'

'We're in for a storm.' The comment was expressionless, but she followed his gaze and spotted the dark clouds massing to the east.

The suddenness and ferocity of the downpour took her by surprise. One moment the sun was on her face, the next raindrops the size of golf balls were pelting down on her, drenching her as thoroughly as a bathroom shower. Guy took the tiller again, grinning at her half-drowned appearance, hair dripping down her back, T-shirt clinging to her breasts.

'Do you want to go below?'

She shook her head. She was wet, but far from cold. She could see a rainbow forming in the cloud-streaked sky. This was her very first tropical rain shower, and she decided that, in spite of acutely disliking her companion, this was an experience definitely not to be missed.

By the time they moored out in Soufrière Bay and prepared the dinghy to row to shore, the sun was shining again, and the air felt fresher. Everything glistened with new intensity. The twin peaks of the Piton volcanoes rose mysteriously, their wooded slopes shadowed purple, above a coastline of green and gold.

She glanced at the dark shape of Guy Sterne at her side, and saw him watching her.

'This is a beautiful place,' he said quietly. 'Don't you think so?'

'I. . .yes.' She found herself caught up in an intensely speculative gaze. The green-grey eyes had a hypnotic quality. Her throat tightened, and she dragged her eyes away.

'Don't be so afraid to drop that prickly guard, Virginia,' he said, that soft tiger-growl in his voice bringing goose-skin to her arms and legs. 'There's nothing immoral about relaxation.'

'I don't recall saying there was. . .'

She was acutely aware of his half-closed eyes watching her mouth as she began arguing. For a fearful moment she thought he was going to lean down and kiss her, and because she had no idea how she would defend herself if he did she shut her eyes tightly, opting for the ostrich technique.

'Are you all right?' His hands were warm and firm on her upper arms, and she caught her breath. The note in his voice wasn't easy to decipher, but his words brought her eyes wide open again. 'You're not about to pass out on me again?'

'I. . .no! I'm fine, really. . .' A wash of unwelcome colour crept into her cheeks. She gave herself a quick mental shake. It was something in the air, she decided, some voodoo spell maybe. Taking a deep breath, she managed a cool smile up at the enigmatic face above her, and took brutal control of her wayward emotions.

Her resentment of Guy Sterne's involvement with her family was somehow getting mixed up with a physical chemistry, she decided uneasily, and she found the latter far more confusing and unnerving. The flashes of hostility between them could only make things worse. From now on, she was going to behave impeccably. She'd be polite and charming if it killed her! Remaining distant and civilised in this man's provocative company was the only way of defusing the physical tension. . .

The sheer beauty of their surroundings helped her to distance herself from the unsettling vibrations between them. The Diamond Mineral Baths were reached through flower-scented botanical gardens, in a densely

wooded gorge. Birds and butterflies flitted round their
heads. Vanilla climbed delicately around the trunks of
cocoa and citrus. Guy proved an excellent guide, laconically volunteering the names of most of the plants and
birds, and conversation remained on an impersonal
monotone.

Even so, Virginia was glad when they finally reached
the baths and found there was a choice of communal
outdoor pools or private indoor ones. She opted for the
safety of the latter. She definitely wasn't about to endure
the intimacy of sharing a pool with Guy Sterne.

The relief of escaping from his company was so intense
that she felt as if she'd been wired up to an electric
charge for the last few hours and someone had finally
taken pity on her and turned off the power.

Ensconsed in the privacy of one of the new modern
bath-rooms, she turned off the tap, lay back in the warm
mineral water, let her whole body go limp, and let her
mind follow suit. Through the haze of steam she contem-
plated nothing much at all, and gradually felt some of
her tension and wariness disperse.

'Definitely an improvement.' Guy Sterne's smile was
dry as she finally emerged to join him by the outdoor
pools, her expression almost serene. 'Would you like a
drink?'

'Mmm. Please.' Her calm, lazy response made him
laugh. While he went to get her a glass of freshly
squeezed lemon and lime juice she tried to resent his
patronising amusement, but failed to summon up
enough ill-feeling to do so.

'Relaxation doesn't look like a problem now.' He eyed
her quizzically across the table as she sipped the
delicious drink and wriggled her toes in reluctant

pleasure. 'Keeping you awake might be the new challenge.'

'Nonsense. The water's very. . .reviving.'

'Good. Do you feel up to some sightseeing?'

She shrugged. 'Why not?'

'But lunch first.'

'Whatever you say.'

She received a suspicious glance at this placid response, but she refused to be drawn. She intended holding on to this new inner peace for as long as she could.

'Well, congratulations,' Guy drawled after lunch, as they drank coffee on the terrace of a restaurant with a panoramic view of the Pitons. Over a delicious meal of freshwater crayfish in lime butter, and a light-as-air mango soufflé, they'd held an impeccably detached, wonderfully calm conversation ranging from Caribbean history to ethnic crafts and design, and discovered common ground on half a dozen other topics including a penchant for the Post-Impressionists, an affinity with the work and designs of William Morris, and a liking for cricket.

'What's that supposed to mean?' The dark green sun umbrella above them threw shadows across Guy's face, but she realised that the teasing gleam had crept back into the narrowed gaze.

'We've spent an hour and a half together without a raised voice or a clenched fist! When you lower the spiky defences a fraction and forget the political soapbox, you're pleasant company!' He grinned blandly. 'Do you want some more coffee?'

'No, thanks.' The defensiveness was back with a

vengeance, but there seemed no way she could control it.

'When you're not spitting venom, or preaching amateur socialism, I've even noticed you're passably attractive,' he persisted teasingly. 'I may revise my previous aversion to redheads!'

The words were lightly spoken, but the darker gleam in his eyes was unmistakably sensual. Her stomach seemed to plummet. She stiffened instinctively.

'Please don't bother to revise any aversions on my account. I'd hate you to waste your time!' she said acidly.

'Do I detect a challenge, Virginia?' Guy's eyes were amused on her shuttered face.

'No! Not in the least!' She drained her coffee, and focused coldly on the towering mountains in the distance. What on earth was the matter with her. Why couldn't she hold her own under this sudden onslaught of innocuous banter? She was behaving like a child.

'You're an interesting paradox, you know.'

'No, I don't know, and I really don't——'

'Ice maiden, with fiery red hair and simmering green eyes!' He was casually waving the waiter over to settle the bill, his voice reflective. 'Touchy feminist with a soft vulnerable smile——'

'Look,' she burst out, goaded beyond control, 'I thought *you* suggested a truce earlier?'

'I hadn't realised I was resuming hostilities!' Guy pointed out blithely. 'I'm just interested to know what goes on beneath that hostile little shell you present to the world, Virginia. Why do you find that so threatening, I wonder?'

Her throat was suddenly dry.

'I'm *so* flattered you want to discover more about me, but there's disappointingly little to discover,' she managed, with an artificially sweet smile, 'And rest assured I don't feel in the least *threatened*. Can we go?'

'Calm down. You can relax again now.' Guy stood up and smiled down at her with such glittering mockery that she wanted to thump him. 'We'll revert to discussing the Post-Impressionists, shall we? And I suppose we'd better go and asphyxiate ourselves up at the sulphur springs. St Lucians get very affronted if you come to Soufrière without seeing their famous sulphur springs!'

He rested his arm lightly along her shoulders as they left the restaurant, and she forced herself to wait a decent interval before ducking lightly away from him, hating the insidious way his touch seemed to affect her.

The rest of the afternoon passed uneasily. She was too preoccupied by her inner turmoil to fully appreciate the bubbling volcanic mud pools in the weird, lunar-like springs. By the time they got back to the *Buccaneer*, the sun was turning pink and orange to usher in another early Caribbean night, and Virginia felt weary with the emotional tension of avoiding either body or eye contact with her companion, and keeping the conversation on a relentlessly impersonal level.

'Don't look so alarmed,' Guy murmured wryly, seeing her sudden concern as he ducked below to turn on some lights. 'The *Buccaneer* has an engine. And I have my yacht master's certificate.'

'I wasn't feeling at all alarmed!' she protested. But the night around them seemed impossibly dark, the stars impossibly high and brilliant. The lights of Soufrière

twinkled a long way off as they set off into the black, and
headed north for Marigot Bay.

'Are you OK?' The silence had stretched out for some
time. 'You're not feeling ill?'

'No. I was just thinking how this feels incred-
ibly. . .atmospheric,' she heard herself admitting reluctantly, waving an arm to encompass the satiny darkness
of the sea all around them, 'I was thinking of the ghosts
of all those Spanish galleons which met a sticky end in
these very waters, hundreds of years ago,' she added,
with a touch of melodrama which made him laugh out
loud.

'Just as I suspected. Under that hard-as-nails,
women's-lib exterior beats the heart of a romantic?'

She felt her cheeks go warmer in the darkness. Hard
as nails? Was that how he saw her? She swallowed
convulsively, unwilling to admit that his judgement hurt.

'It's the West Indies that's romantic, not me. This
whole area feels weighed down with. . .ghosts and
legends and old feuds and betrayals. It's *captivating*!'

She spoke with such soft intensity that he stared at
her for a long, thoughtful moment. She was aware of his
scrutiny, but the shadowy darkness hid his eyes. She
couldn't see what would undoubtedly be the cynical
mockery there. And she didn't care anyway. She'd never
before felt such a surge of creative stimulation. The urge
to translate her emotions into some tangible piece of
artwork made her itch to get pencil to paper.

She was still so entranced by the timeless atmosphere
of their night-time sail back round the island that it was
strange to hear Lucy's familiar voice on the telephone
that night.

'You sound very calm, bearing in mind this mix-up

you've landed in!' Lucy sounded impishly curious about the situation, as well as suitably apologetic. 'How are you getting on with Guy?'

'As well as can be expected.'

'Oh, dear. And no doubt you can't say too much, because Guy's around!'

'Correct.' Virginia shifted self-consciously on the blue and yellow sofa, forcing a polite smile as Guy strolled past. He was wearing disreputable-looking denim bermudas. A white T-shirt clung faithfully to the contoured steel of his pectoral muscles. She watched him sprawl in a cane chair on the terrace, light a cigar, and pick up a book, uncaring of the many and varied insects homing in on the light above him. While her eyes were drawn to him, Tara emerged from another of the doors leading on to the terrace, clad in a saffron-yellow mini-skirt and tiny crop-top. She bent over him, her long dark hair brushing his face. She whispered something, and Guy grinned and shrugged, put down the book and stood up. Together they went back inside the villa. She heard the french door into Guy's bedroom close quietly behind them.

Virginia felt frozen to the spot, unable to move a muscle. The surge of undefinable emotion she experienced was almost paralysing.

'I hope you appreciate I'm burning the midnight oil to ring you tonight,' Lucy's voice persisted from its far-off country, 'And all I'm getting is monosyllables for my trouble! I said, where were you earlier? I've been trying to ring all evening!'

Virginia made a supreme effort to pull herself together. She'd forgotten the time difference. Half-past seven here meant past midnight over in England.

'Sorry, Lucy. We sailed round to Soufrière. Guy had a theory that the mineral baths might speed up my convalescence. Wasn't Tara here?'

'No one answered. Who's Tara, anyway?'

'Guy Sterne's girlfriend.'

There was a blank silence, then Lucy laughed, rather nervously.

'That makes sense, I suppose. . . Everyone in London was wondering why Guy left his fiancée on her own, and flew off to the Caribbean on the spur of the moment. . .'

'His fiancée. . .?' Why should it *matter*? she demanded silently, clamping an iron hand on her wayward reactions. He could have six fiancées, and it would make no difference to her.

'She's his boss's daughter, too. You'd better swear an oath of secrecy, or Nicola Schreider will *not* be amused to find out Guy's been playing away even before they're married!'

'No. I don't suppose she would be.' Virginia blinked into space, her brain reeling at this unexpected line of information. So the Schreider of Schreider Sterne Inc. was older, with a daughter old enough for Guy Sterne to plan on marrying. . .poor girl, Virginia reflected pityingly. She imagined herself being vulnerable to the kind of pain Guy Sterne would be capable of inflicting, and she shivered inside. . .

Snapping guiltily out of her reverie, she enquired after Lucy's health, and the state of the business. The answers did little to cheer her up. Lucy had to stay in bed as much as possible on doctor's orders, Dad was spending more and more time on the golf course and in the pub to escape from what he called the 'pressures', and Charles was in an increasingly pessimistic mood about the future of Chester's.

'I feel so *guilty* lying around out here in the Caribbean, while you're ill, and Charles and Dad are worried out of their minds!'

'Don't start that again! You really *need* that holiday, so make the most of it! Just do us a favour and come home fully recovered, Virgie, darling! Look, I'd better go, I can hardly keep my eyes open! Dad and Charles send their love. They went down to the Crown and Trumpet a couple of hours ago. . .'

'I see. So the landlord's holding an after-hours booze-up as usual!'

'Quite likely!'

'Well, give them my love when you see them. Night, Lucy darling. Take care. . .'

'And you. Have fun with the divine Guy, and no more fainting fits!'

She had to restrain herself from slamming the receiver down with shameful violence. The divine Guy! More like the diabolical Guy, Virginia thought sourly, going distractedly into the kitchen and pouring herself a glass of mango juice.

To steer her mind off the goings-on in Guy's bedroom, she found her drawing things and began sketching. Taking the germ of an idea from the exotic blend of shapes and colours and textures she'd absorbed during their day out, she worked slowly and painstakingly to create several tiny, intricate designs.

She was so absorbed in the task that she hardly noticed time passing. She didn't realise that Guy Sterne had joined her in the sitting-room until he spoke from behind her chair.

'Those are very good.'

It was a huge effort not to cover her work quickly, like
a secretive schoolgirl. Instead she glanced at him with a
blithe smile which she hoped disguised her true feelings,
and carried on inking in colour.

'Thanks. . .'

'Inspiration from the Caribbean?' The wry smile
accompanying the words made her throat tighten.
Doggedly she kept her head down over the jewel-
coloured designs, trying to concentrate, but after another
few seconds she gave up and laid down her pen with
elaborate resignation.

'Don't stop.' His grin was lopsided, 'People who work
with their tongue between their teeth invariably rivet my
attention.'

She compressed her lips. 'Riveting your attention
wasn't my aim, although you'd find that hard to believe,
of course!'

'Of course. I need a lot of attention. I was a badly
neglected baby.'

She glared at him in defensive exasperation. When he
was in this mood, it was mysteriously hard to resist Guy
Sterne. Sprawled on the opposite sofa, he was the
epitome of relaxation. His dark limbs gleamed like oiled
gold beneath the faded bermudas and T-shirt. Glancing
around, she deduced from the sounds drifting from the
kitchen that Tara was preparing a meal. From bed to
kitchen. Fulfilling her prescribed roles with subservient
perfection. She suppressed the angry thoughts. It was
none of her business how a girl like Tara chose to
organise her life.

But her sense of being an embarrassing extra grew
depressingly stronger.

'How does a drawing like that get to be printed on yards of Sarah Chester furnishing fabric?' He nodded to the artwork on the table, eyes narrowed with apparent interest.

'I don't design for Sarah Chester's,' she retorted calmly, slipping the pages into a folder and closing it decisively. 'I think I'll get an early night. . .'

'But if, for example, Chester's wanted to print fabric using those designs?'

She gave him a sharp look. Was he just making polite conversation with his uninvited guest, or was he pumping her for information?

'Chester's has its own design management team. And a computer-aided textile design system. . .' she began formally, keen to grab the chance to put the firm in a good light. He held up his hand to stop her.

'I don't want the full PR spiel, Virginia. I'm just curious about the methods. *How* do you get a little drawing like that on to thousands of metres of fabric?'

'OK. A computer separates the different colours. And rationalises pattern repeats and so on.' She worked hard to keep the cool defensiveness out of her voice. If Guy Sterne was showing an interest in the procedures and systems of Sarah Chester's, it might be a good sign, mightn't it? 'A complicated sort of photographic process transfers the design on to mesh screen rollers in Chester's engraving department. The screens are slotted on to an amazing new printer which cost the company an arm and a leg a couple of years ago. It can print up to twelve colours at the same time. . .'

She hesitated, almost mesmerised by the piercing concentration fixed on her. Guy Sterne gave the unnerving impression of a computer-style brain which was recording every word for future reference. No wonder he was such a top dog in the City if he wielded this calibre of authority merely via the passive act of listening!

'Go on?'

'That's it, really. They pipe the right dyes into the screens. They feed some material through the printer. They switch on and. . .away you go!'

'Interesting.'

'Presumably you could pay a flying visit to Sarah Chester Fabrics printing plant and see for yourself some time?' The faint note of sarcasm seemed lost on him.

'There's a batik factory on St Lucia,' he continued calmly, 'you might find it interesting to see a primitive style of fabric printing, compare it with all this high-tech stuff Chester's handle. I'll take you there tomorrow, if you like.'

'I really don't want to take up any more of your time. . .'

Despite strenuous efforts to disguise it, her hostility was showing.

Guy's gaze narrowed disconcertingly on her set face. With a fluid movement he stood up and came across to tilt her rigid chin up with his thumb.

'Hey. . .' It was that dark, unbearable cat-purr again, sending tremors along her nerve-ends. 'What happened to the romantic dreaming about sunken ships and old buried gold?'

'Don't *touch* me!' The words, softly intense, were out before she could stop them. She twisted away from his hand, but he caught hold of her arm as she tried to push past him, swinging her round to face him, pulling her against him.

'What's so bad about being touched, Virginia?' He

sounded thoughtful, his voice huskier. 'You spent all afternoon twitching like a frightened animal if I dared put my hand on your arm——'

'Let me *go*!'

Struggling this close to the muscular height of Guy Sterne was a big mistake, she dimly reflected, because each fresh body contact was a torment. She'd changed her earlier shorts and T-shirt for a cool beige wrap-style cotton dress, belted at the waist with a strip of tan leather. The cross-over neck gaped treacherously as she fought silently to free herself, revealing a smooth swell of breast without the support of a bra. His body heat was overwhelming. There was a subtle lemon-musk fragrance to his skin which made her head swim. By the time he'd captured her flailing arms, and crushed her hips close enough to minimise damage from her kicking feet, she was shivering so convulsively that she felt almost feverish.

'Just calm down. . .'

'What's the matter with you?' she fired at him furiously. 'Do you have such an inflated idea of your own sex appeal you think you can grab any woman who happens to be to hand?'

'What's that supposed to mean?' he taunted softly. 'How many women am I supposed to have grabbed tonight?'

'I'm not *blind*! What about Tara?' All her nerve-endings were raw. Six feet of solid, sinewy muscle slammed against her was swamping her senses.

'Have I "grabbed" Tara tonight?'

He was so mocking, so tormentingly cool. Virginia's habitual quiet reserve deserted her.

'I'm not interested in your. . .*lascivious* lifestyle!' she spat fiercely, punching at his chest but failing to free herself, 'But I'm sure your fiancée back in England would be!'

There was a resounding pause. Her heart was beating so fast that she felt out of breath.

'Just for the record,' he said at last, in a dangerously soft drawl, 'Tara is my housekeeper, Virginia.'

'Really? And I'm the Duchess of York!'

He examined her objectively for several minutes.

'Your hair's the right shade of Titian. But there the similarity ends.'

Their eyes clashed and locked. Guy Sterne's eyes held a glitter of amusement, but a darker emotion she saw in the pale green-grey brought colour sweeping up her neck to her face.

'You're very liberal with your criticism, Virginia,' he drawled huskily. 'But you're hardly the model of perfection. You give out conflicting signals, did you know that. . .?'

'No! That's not true. . .' She felt sick as an echo of the past caught up with her. Mortimer had once said something along those lines. . .

'If I kiss you, will I be prosecuted for sexual harassment when we get back to England?'

'Don't be so stupid. . .' She was marshalling all her reserves of anger and distaste, but they were being insidiously undermined by a sensation she couldn't begin to describe. 'Besides, you don't go for redheads, you told me you don't, and you're engaged to be married, and what about Ta——?'

He cut off the rest of the frantic protest with his mouth, wrenching her against him and covering her angrily parted lips with his own. She shut her eyes, unsure if she was trying to blot out the unexpected hunger in his kiss, or opting for her ostrich trick again and trying to pretend this wasn't happening to her.

And it wasn't happening the way she'd imagined. . .abruptly, she realised that being kissed by Guy Sterne was nothing remotely like being kissed by any other man she'd ever known in her life. The heat in the room was already intensely humid. But the heat generated between them sent the temperature rocketing wildly. Her body seemed to leap into overdrive. The thrust of his invasive tongue was unbelievably erotic. . .it was frightening, and exciting, and even the grim memory of Mortimer couldn't shake off the shivers of reaction in her stomach.

With a low gasp she let her fingers slide up over the daunting hardness of his shoulders, touch the short, thick hair at his nape. . .he moved his hands down to her hips, in a quick convulsive movement, crushing her against him. He was rock hard, fully aroused beneath the rough denim of his bermudas, and she froze, beginning to struggle in nameless fear. . .completely new emotions were being aroused much too fast. She was too swamped with sensation to reason logically, but some far recess of her brain was screaming out warnings, remembering past experiences. . .

'Dinner's ready. . .' Tara's warm, honeyed tones broke the treacherous spell. They fell apart, breathing fiercely, as if they'd run a race. Appalled at herself, Virginia spun round to face the other girl, read the anguished look in the charcoal eyes. So Tara was just Guy Sterne's housekeeper? She pushed blindly past Guy, and made a desperate bolt for the door.

'You two go ahead,' she managed to say chokingly, her throat aching with self-disgust. 'I'm going to bed. . .'

Escaping to her room, she shut the door with careful control behind her, then wedged a chair under the handle with trembling fingers before sinking weakly on to the seat and burying her hot face in her hands.

CHAPTER FIVE

'WE NEED to talk,' Guy informed her calmly in the morning, across the white table on the terrace. The brilliance of the blue and gold morning, the fragrance of fresh-ground coffee, the tranquil pool and bewitching glimpse of blue sea beyond—it was all in marked contrast to her bleak mood.

'I don't think so.' Virginia buttered another roll, and sent up a silent vote of thanks for whoever had invented sun-glasses. It was debatable if she could have faced Guy Sterne across the breakfast table without them.

'I'd rather forget all about last night,' she continued coldly, trying to avoid the mockery in his narrowed eyes. 'Besides, it doesn't matter. Your morals are your own business. . .'

'You've lost me.'

'What I can't understand is why you were so keen for me to stay here, in the circumstances. . .'

'In what circumstances, Virginia?'

His eyes were half closed, but there was a brilliant challenge in the cool gaze. Her throat dried. Did he have to fix her with that piercing scrutiny? It threw her train of thought completely. And it brought back last night's powerful sensations, steaming through her system like an express train.

'I mean. . .' She swallowed hard, unsure if she had the nerve to go ahead. The memory of the pain in Tara's eyes last night decided her. Did he *really* expect her to

81

believe that Tara was only the housekeeper? And did he have to flaunt his sexual prowess with her as well, just because she happened to be female, and happened to be there?

'Look. . .' she began wearily, returning his gaze with her most cynical and uninterested. 'Whatever's going on here, count me out. OK? I can see your dilemma. You've got your *fiancée* at home, for the serious, lifestyle-building stuff, and you've got the delectable Tara out here, for fun and relaxation. Fine. Then I show up and complicate matters. . .'

'And, being the modern-day equivalent of Casanova, I decide to add you to this impressive circle of conquests?'

Her cheeks were growing hotter. The mocking drawl in his voice was making her feel like a five-year-old.

'Goodness knows,' she said crossly, draining her coffee cup, and grating back her chair. 'I haven't a clue why you behave in the way you appear to behave and I honestly don't give a damn. . .'

'So there's nothing I can say to redeem myself?'

'I don't want to hear it. I'm not *interested* in your personal affairs, do you understand?'

'But you are interested in my business affairs.' The flat assertion made her stop in mid-escape, and glance at him uncertainly.

'I couldn't fail to be, could I?' She thrust her hands into the pockets of her peach-pattern culotte-shorts, and battled with her errant temper. 'In view of your imminent involvement with my father's company.'

'Which you resent.' He nodded thoughtfully, standing up too, dauntingly attractive in black chino shorts and matching polo shirt. 'We're both in a dilemma then, aren't we?'

'I'm afraid I don't foll——'

'In fact, this could be "check-mate", when we consider all the options,' he cut in, his tone ominously conversational. 'The way I see it, I have to be wary of upsetting you, in case you go home and tell this fiancée of mine all about my wicked Caribbean love-nest. And you have to be wary of upsetting me in case I'm planning on the wholesale destruction of Sarah Chester Fabrics. Have I got this right so far?'

'You might find this amusing. I don't!'

'Did I say I was amused?'

He was much too close for her peace of mind now. Wildly she glanced around for Tara, but after an early swim she'd disappeared.

'The implication that I'd stoop to. . .to *blackmail* I resent very much! I hope your fiancée finds out what sort of man you are before it's too late, but she won't hear anything from *me*!'

'You're bad for a man's ego, Virginia. I flew out here feeling tired and overworked, but relatively sound in the moral-fibre department. Since I met you my self-esteem has sunk to an all-time low!'

She flinched under the merciless sarcasm in his smile.

'My heart bleeds for you. Why *did* you fly out here? Apart from the obvious reason?'

'The obvious reason?'

'Tara, naturally! She doesn't look like the kind of girl men want to be parted from for too long!'

'True. She doesn't, does she? She does have a great technique in the bedroom, I admit, but she's not the reason I come out to St Lucia. . .'

'But you admit. . .you. . .you go to bed with her!'

He fingered his jaw thoughtfully, eyes glittering at the scarlet patches in her cheeks.

'Not in the way you think. Tara is a masseuse. Not the sleazy variety, either. She's very proudly qualified as an aromatherapist. She does things with *neroli* and *ylang ylang* which can turn a man's knees to water. . .'

'Oh, go to hell!' she spat, unable to hide her sudden shiver of emotion. She turned to march away but got only a few inches before she was hauled back. The grip on her arm didn't hurt, exactly, but it was firm enough to rivet her to the spot.

'Listen, will you?' His tone was suddenly low and impatient. The teasing smile was gone. The hard glitter in his eyes was mesmerising. 'Give that suspicious, mixed-up little brain a rest. The truth may not be what you want to hear, but I don't find this situation funny any longer——'

'Will you let go of my arm, please?'

'Only if you stand still and listen.'

Dry-mouthed, she nodded abruptly. He dropped his hand from her arm and she rubbed the spot resentfully.

'Tara looks after Hummingbird House for me. She's a very competent, well-paid housekeeper. She even acts as a secretary for me occasionally. That's all.'

'I *saw* you go into your bedroom with her, last night! You must think I'm blind. . .'

She felt weak with panic. How had this agonising confrontation arisen? It was too mortifying for words, and it intensified the vulnerable feeling she'd been experiencing around Guy Sterne. Because it had suddenly occurred to her that Guy Sterne was bothering to justify himself like this only because his relationship with

Nicola Schreider was threatened if he didn't. Otherwise she felt certain he'd dismiss the whole embarrassing situation with a careless sneer. But *she* was acting like a jealous girlfriend. . .this was insane. . .

'Tara is a qualified aromatherapist.' He was watching her face intently, and a dark gleam of unholy amusement returned as he saw her cynical disbelief. 'Believe what you like,' he added with a shrug.

'Tara is madly in love with you, not that it's any of my business,' she countered icily.

'What makes you say that?'

'I've seen the way she looks at you! Oh, for heaven's sake, why are we having this stupid conversation?' she exploded, green eyes blazing hostility.

'That's what interests me.'

'Well, we both know why, of course!' she answered herself furiously. 'You're trying to protect your relationship with your fiancée. And I'm trying to get it through your arrogant skull that I'm not in the market for a casual roll in the hay just because we happen to be sharing a villa for a few days!'

'Is that why?'

'Well, isn't it?'

The dark face was a bland, maddening mask. A long pause stretched out, and she realised she was shaking all over with emotion after the argument.

'Time to call another truce.' His voice was sardonic. 'Time to resume the guided tour of the island, Miss Chester. Let's sail round to Castries.' He saw her open her mouth to argue, and his eyes hardened a fraction in wry self-mockery. 'You can tell me all about Sarah Chester's range of products on the way. Since your father's company is the only reason you're deigning to

associate with riff-raff like me, you might as well grab
your chances while you can.'

She glared at him helplessly.

'Are you accusing me of. . .of *using* this mix-up to try
to gain some advantage for Chester Fabrics?'

He laughed suddenly, his gaze very keen on her
flushed face. 'I think the notion has crossed your mind,'
he taunted softly.

Their eyes locked, stormy green riveted by cool grey.
The silence hung endlessly, vibrating with unspoken
tensions. Her blood seemed to be pumping through her
veins at twice the normal speed.

The wry twist of amusement around his lips finally
proved impossible to resist. Her deeply buried sense of
humour came to her rescue.

'I suppose we could have another go at being friendly
holiday acquaintances?' she suggested, slightly unsteadily. 'As long as. . . I mean, if you'll promise not to
haul me into another clinch?'

'You didn't seem to be complaining at the time.'

Virginia took a deep breath. Straight speaking was in
order, she decided.

'I'm not saying kissing you wasn't quite pleasant, as
kisses go,' she informed him as calmly as she could,
desperately trying to disguise the way her heart was
pounding with fear as she recalled her reactions to that
kiss. 'I'm just telling you that. . .that I'm not interested.
I mean. . . I realise that to a man like you this situation
is probably an open invitation to a spot of casual sex,
even if generally you don't fancy redheads, as you so
gallantly pointed out when we first met. . .' She was
gabbling now, she dimly recognised, but it was too late
to stem the flow of words. 'But. . .oh, heavens, this

sounds arrogant, as if I'm some irresistible Lolita or something. . .but I wouldn't want you getting any ideas about me while we're thrown together like this. . .'

The glitter of mockery was back with a vengeance, with a darker glint of what could have been anger in his eyes carefully screened by a rakish smile.

'My heart is broken,' he assured her with emphasis, crashing his hand to his chest with wry drama. 'But from now on I'll do my best to be as chaste as a Catholic priest.'

A distinctly uneasy peace reigned for the rest of the day. But as the hours passed, and the relatively impersonal topic of Chester's market share, company structure and ailing profit figures gave way to a general, easygoing discussion about Caribbean history and culture, Virginia was aware of a slight relaxation in atmosphere.

Maybe the fraught confrontation earlier had defused some of the tension building up between them. Or had it been between them, or only in her own highly tuned emotions? She wasn't quite sure any longer. Anyway, she'd said her piece. Guy Sterne's relationships with other women were no concern of hers. At least he now knew there was no question of any kind of casual relationship with *her*. . .

And she might not like Guy Sterne very much, but he was curiously easy to talk to.

In Castries they strolled through the busy streets, bought bread, cheese and fruit for a picnic, and drank iced rum under the shade of a café umbrella, where they amicably discussed St Lucia's long tug-of-war between French and English, and tried to decipher the local French patois being spoken all around them.

In the duty-free shopping centre she noticed a couple

of English girls buying jewellery and leather handbags, who ogled Guy with open interest. Guy's cool, wolfish enjoyment of their flirtatious smiles triggered another maelstrom of confusion inside her. Was she actually feeling *possessive* about her companion?

This perfidious inner reaction drove her into ferocious silence as they headed back down the coast again, berating her stupidity as she watched the lush green hills glide by.

If she was seriously letting herself fall for this man's serpentine charm, then all she could think was that the glandular fever had affected her brain cells as well as her blood cells. For heaven's sake, she lectured herself despairingly, he was two-timing a fiancée back in England, and if last night's incident had been any indication he was quite prepared to embark on a brief dalliance with her as well as Tara. . .

The man's amorality in business dealings spilled over into his personal life. He was poised to carve up Chester's and collect his profits without a backward glance. . .he was bad news. . .

And, on top of that, he frightened her. . .physically, sexually. . .the experience with Mortimer was still so raw and painful. Feelings like those feelings Guy Sterne had roused in her last night were anathema. They could only lead down a particularly humiliating blind alley she'd vowed she'd avoid at all costs. . .

'You're very quiet again.' Guy's eyes were screened by the Raybans as they dropped anchor off a deserted palm-fringed bay, and rowed over to a deserted white crescent of sand to unload the picnic hamper. 'Are we overdoing the sightseeing?'

'No. . .it must be the rum. I feel pole-axed.'

Guy spread out a huge sky-blue towel, a few feet from the edge of the sea, and rammed an emerald and white sun umbrella firmly into the sand beside it.

'It's the humidity. Sit down. Relax. I'll be head waiter. Would *mademoiselle* care for chilled white Californian Chardonnay with her bread and cheese?'

'First I must cool down. I'm going for a swim.' Suddenly it was imperative to escape from his disturbing nearness. Discarding the culotte-shorts, she ran down into the water clad in her olive-green one-piece. Scoop-necked, and cut high on the hip, at least it felt safer than a bikini. The water was deliciously refreshing. A powerful splash beside her told her Guy had dived in too, scything rapidly out towards the moored ketch then arcing back round to the shore in that stylish front crawl. She felt irritated by her lack of fitness. A year ago she'd have been able to race him out to the ketch, maybe even climbed on deck and dived off. . .

'Don't worry about it,' he told her calmly, when she confided her frustration. 'Take things slowly. You'll be fully recovered before you know it.'

'This is the knowledgeable doctor's son speaking?'

'Just common sense. Just like it's common sense not to lie in the Caribbean sun too long.'

She was face down on the towel, letting the sun scorch her dry. Face turned on one arm, she risked a glance along the muscular length of the body stretched a couple of feet away from her, the briefest black trunks accentuating the dusky, even tan of his skin. When her eyes moved back up to his face, she realised he was watching her covert examination, his heavy-lidded gaze amused. She blinked and scoured her brain desperately for a

neutral topic of conversation to deflect his attention, but
the question which emerged proved far from neutral.

'Do you see much of your family?' She didn't know
why she felt compelled to probe. But, for some reason,
the answer didn't surprise her.

'Up until recently, as little as possible.'

'That sounds rather. . .bitter?' She was remembering
his expression the night she'd blacked out, when he'd
first mentioned his father.

'We can't all play happy families. A lot of families are
hell. You're lucky if you survive them at all.' The bland
lack of intonation didn't fool her. Guy Sterne didn't just
avoid seeing his family, he didn't like talking about them
either. Curiosity deepened.

'Were you an only child?'

He gave a short, humourless laugh, and levered
himself up to investigate the hamper.

'Until I was twelve. Then out of the hat my parents
produced an older sister. It took me quite a while to
cope with the shock.'

The wry self-mockery was stronger. Frowning, she sat
up cross-legged on the towel under the shade of the
umbrella, and accepted a wedge of cheese and some
crusty bread.

'How could they produce an *older* sister?'

'A spectre from their past. They'd met while they were
both studying. My father as a medical student, my
mother as a psychologist. A baby then would have been
impossible for them both. They had it adopted. Later on
they married. I was another accident, I imagine. Only
they decided to hang on to me.'

'And she. . . I mean your sister. . .tracked your
parents down when she was old enough?'

'That's it.'

'What a bombshell!'

'The irony is, Claire's just like them. She's a social worker. The caring professional. I'd already given up trying to please my father. I resisted the "clone" pressure. . .'

'You mean he wanted you to follow him into his profession? Or something similar?'

'Quite.'

'So instead you got a job in the City?'

'Neat, wasn't it? Can I ask the motive for this interrogation, Miss Chester?'

'Sorry. . . I wasn't interrogating. I was just interested. . .'

'And I've been blurting out my life story like there's no tomorrow. You must be a deceptively good listener.'

'That sounds a back-handed compliment!'

'Deceptive because of all your tirading and crusading.' He was uncorking the bottle of wine, his expression unreadable. 'I'd have classed you as too wrapped up in your own virtuous opinions to be much good at listening to other people's.'

'Thanks. There's nothing *wrong* with virtue!'

'Only when it's misdirected. Then it turns into self-righteous hypocrisy.'

There was a short, tense silence.

'I am not self-righteous. And I loathe hypocrisy,' she retorted finally, her voice clipped with suppressed emotion. 'Maybe you just bring out the worst in me!'

'I see. My fault again?' It was a sardonic jibe, but as she reached out to accept the proffered wine she met his eyes, and felt jolted by the gleam of warmth she detected in the grey-green depths.

Taking a deep swallow of the wine, she glanced away, watching a large rigged sailboat as it glided by, packed with holidaymakers, distant strains of steel band music and laughter drifting over on the wind.

'You said you didn't see much of your family until recently. What changed?'

'My mother was ill.'

'Oh. I'm sorry. . .'

'She's all right now. There were some. . .compensations that came out of the experience of sitting round a hospital bed with my father and my sister.'

'You patched things up?'

'After a fashion.' He grinned suddenly, disarming her with the brilliance of his smile. 'Now it's your turn.'

'I beg your pardon?'

'Your turn to answer questions, with the truth, the whole truth and nothing but the truth.'

She shrugged slightly, and laughed. 'There's nothing particularly interesting to find out, I assure you. If you've known Charles and Lucy for years, then you'll know pretty well all there is to know about my background. . .'

'Who's the man, Virginia?'

'What?' Heat crept up her neck in spite of her rigid composure.

'The man responsible for this ice queen act of yours?'

'I haven't the faintest idea what you——'

'Just a minute.' He put down his glass and took hers from fingers which were inexplicably trembling, then twisted her round to inspect her back, 'You've had your back in the sun. You're burning. Turn round, I'll put some sun lotion on for you.'

After a few moments of frozen hesitation, she realised that to refuse his offer would only reinforce his current impression that she was a frigid little puritan with hang-ups about physical contact. With a sinking feeling she nodded and shifted her position obediently.

'You were going to say you haven't the faintest idea what I'm talking about,' he continued softly, slipping the swimsuit straps off her shoulders. She bit her lip hard as cool sun lotion was smoothed on to her hot skin. 'But you have. You know what I'm talking about, Virginia. Admit it.'

She clung to the front of her costume, gritting her teeth as he widened the circle of massage, smoothing the cream over her shoulders and down towards the small of her back.

'Something or someone has frightened you off men. I don't believe it's just me you've taken a violent dislike to——'

'Your ego wouldn't let you,' she agreed violently.

'You're not rating too well in the truth stakes, Virginia. What if I told you Nicola Schreider is my *ex*-fiancée? That this prim disapproving act isn't necessary on that score? Would you let me kiss you again?'

'It's perfectly possible to take a violent dislike to someone on sight!' She was shaking all over. He must be able to feel it. The mortifying thought occurred to her that he was playing games, that he somehow had telepathic powers and could read every angry, frightened, confused, cowardly thought scurrying through her brain. . .

'In that case, it must be possible to be violently *attracted* to someone on sight. Do you think?'

The soft drawl was at its most disturbing. So much

for his promised imitation of a Catholic priest, she reflected bitterly. The sensuality in his voice was deliberate.

She closed her eyes. Shivers of reaction were coursing through her whole body at the rhythmic touch of his fingers on her skin.

'I think I've got enough sun lotion on me,' she said, her voice intense. 'And I've had enough food and enough wine. Do you think we could go back to the villa?'

'Sure. Why not?' With casual expertise, he slid her straps back into place, and moved away from her. It was only then she realised she'd been holding her breath. 'Tara's performing at the marina hotel tonight. I said we'd go and watch her.'

'Performing?' She helped pack the hamper, avoiding his eyes as if her life depended on it.

'She's a limbo dancer.' Guy was casually detached again. 'We'll have dinner there tonight. Watch the cabaret. You'll enjoy it.'

Would she? An evening in Guy's company, trying to hide this new throb of awareness which was beginning to throw an entirely different light on her gruesome experience with Mortimer? An evening spent watching the beautiful Tara as a limbo dancer? The prospect, thought Virginia desperately, as they steered the *Buccaneer* back to Marigot Bay, sounded like a refined form of torture.

CHAPTER SIX

THE rhythmic pulsing of the steel band was mesmerising. To the rapid, repetitive beat two glistening bodies were contorting themselves into an impossible position, their backs horizontal to the floor and no more than a foot from it. Their legs entwined, like some exotic two-headed carnival monster in skin-tight red, yellow and blue costumes, the limbo dancers were gyrating their way skilfully beneath a burning pole.

The hotel nightclub was packed with guests, avidly watching the show, most of the women in glamorous evening outfits which almost rivalled the exotic plumage of the limbo costumes. Virginia glanced ruefully down at her own outfit. Her casual white T-shirt dress, belted at the waist, had a button-opening at the scoop-neck, and it was decorated on back and chest with another of her own leaf and peach prints. But she was definitely outshone by the peacock colours and silky materials of her companions. But then she hadn't packed with a hectic night-life in mind, had she? She pushed a slightly unsteady hand through her shoulder-length cloud of freshly washed curls, and fervently wished herself elsewhere.

Guy glanced at her, his mouth twisted in a mocking smile.

'Enjoying it?'

She took a gulp of her drink, and nodded abruptly. What *was* the matter with her tonight? Why couldn't she

just relax and enjoy the evening, like everyone else? But
she was strung up inside. She felt jittery and tense and
ready to explode. The outward calm she was managing
to project was achieved only by a supreme effort of will-
power.

The pair cleared the pole and sprang upright at last.
A slight wisp of smoke came from the back of the man's
hair where the flames had scorched him. Tara, clad in a
tight yellow leotard and matching ruffled skirt, bowed
deeply amidst the applause. Her male partner looked
like a jungle bird in his vivid plumage, ruffles from knee
to ankle, and from upper arm to wrist. Teeth flashing
very white in his mahogany, sweat-beaded face, he ran
lightly over to talk to the band and Tara came barefoot
over to their table.

'Did you like it?' She was looking at Guy, voice soft,
eyes caressing.

'I liked it.'

'We're going to do a contest for the guests.' She
grinned, happiness radiating from her now that she'd
received Guy's approval. Virginia had a sick feeling in
her stomach. 'You'll have a go, won't you?'

The charcoal-brown eyes flicked quickly and dismissively over Virginia, lingering admiringly on Guy's lean
hardness. Khaki chinos and a matching short-sleeved
shirt skimmed the muscular angles of his body to
perfection. He looked. . .taut, Virginia registered in a
detached way. He looked almost as tense as she felt. It
reminded her of the first time she'd seen him. He
probably worked hard at that tough, cynical look, she
decided irritably. Practised in front of the mirror.

Then she decided she'd imagined his tension. The
next minute, he was the teasing, confident extrovert

who'd calmly stripped off in front of her in his bedroom that night.

'Sure, I'm game if you are!' He turned that lop-sided grin towards Virginia, sho shrank into her chair, appalled.

'Watch out, Virginia. Guy's *red* hot at limbo, believe me!' Tara's soft drawl was full of worshipful admiration.

Feeling like the maiden aunt, too rigid with self-consciousness to be persuaded to join in, Virginia miserably sipped more rum and watched the frivolity grow wilder and wilder. After a while it grew apparent that Tara's verdict on Guy was fairly accurate. With daunting suppleness and muscle-power he somehow managed to make each successive reduction in the pole's height look easy to clear, and because he was obviously a fellow tourist queues of hopefuls fell flat on their backs trying to emulate his skill. The atmosphere of the evening turned into one big party.

'Quite the life and soul, aren't you?' She smiled blandly, as they walked back up to Hummingbird House through the velvety darkness.

'I've always had a deplorable tendency to exhibitionism,' Guy agreed, his deep voice full of laughter. 'But you need to loosen up. Inside that repressed little shell something tells me there's a wild, passionate woman begging to be released.'

'Oh, for heaven's sake! You sound like someone out of a corny film!'

The telephone was ringing as they approached the house. Hovering long enough to make sure it wasn't for her, she left him talking in clipped, terse monosyllables and slipped away quietly to her bedroom, trying to suppress her curiosity about the caller. It was really no concern of hers whether it was business or personal. It was just that it was intriguingly difficult to tell if he was issuing blunt ultimatums to a financial contact, or responding to some emotional problem at the other end of the line. . .

She was relieved to gain the sanctuary of her room, and shut the door safely behind her. One way or another it had been quite a day, she decided, cooling down under the shower before she collapsed on to her bed. In fact, ever since she'd arrived she'd been constantly battling, without really being a hundred per cent sure what she was battling against.

She pushed her damp curls from her face, and went to open the french doors to let in what wind there was tonight. The pool lay dark, cool and inviting beyond the terrace. The air hung thick and humid. Maybe there was a storm brewing.

Retreating to lie on her bed, she tossed restlessly. What *was* she so tense about? she wondered, trying to delve into the confusion in her own mind. Was it knowing Guy was capable of wielding ruthless power over Sarah Chester's? Or was it her growing fear that he might wield another kind of power?

She shivered slightly, despite the heat. The touch of his hands on her back that afternoon. . .she'd been gripped by such a war of reaction inside her. Aghast at her line of thought, she sat up abruptly, staring at her shadowy reflection in the mirror opposite the bed. This was unbearable. And it was. . .illogical. After Mortimer's crass behaviour, she'd felt deep-frozen inside. Not even very kind, very polite young men in her year at art school had so much as thawed one tiny corner of her iced-up emotions. So why now? Why the wrong man, wrong in every possible way? How in the world could a worthless louse like Guy Sterne melt her into this uncomfortable aching longing?

In slight panic, she climbed off the bed and swopped her jade cotton nightshirt for the first swimsuit which emerged from her case. It was a gold one, with cool lacing at breast and thighs. Securing her hair in a black band, she padded silently into the warmth of the night and headed for the pool. If she didn't swim off some of this electric energy building up inside her, there could be St Lucia's first case of spontaneous combustion, she decided wryly.

The water was cool silk against her skin. Summoning all her reserves, she swam forcefully down the whole length of the pool, and back again, gradually realising that she felt fitter than she had done for ages. She hadn't had a headache today, in spite of the thundery heat. She didn't feel quite so limp and wilting. . .

Guy was sitting at the pool's edge as she swam back to the shallow end. Her heart did an annoying lurch at the sight of him, long legs dangling in the water, his face too deeply shadowed for her to decipher his mood.

'I was too hot. . .' she found herself explaining shortly. 'I thought a swim might help.'

He was regarding her with unnerving concentration, until she felt she wanted to duck down under the water, fearing her swimsuit was see-through or something. . .

'Do you mind if I join you?' The drawl was clipped, detached. It didn't sound like a voice full of seductive threats. . .

'It's your pool.'

'True. I thought you might panic if I suddenly loomed up beside you in the darkness.'

He stood up and walked down to the deep end as he spoke, then he dived in, surfacing at least halfway down the pool, then covering several more lengths in a leisurely crawl. As he reached her side, the sky above them lit up with a vivid flash of lightning. Almost instantaneously, thunder cracked deafeningly overhead. She wasn't normally afraid of thunderstorms, she chided herself crossly, as alarm pulsed through her body. But then she wasn't normally in a swimming-pool, in the heart of the sub-tropical Caribbean. The elements seemed very awesome.

Lightning flashed again, brilliant as a fluorescent light. Guy caught sight of her expression, and closed the distance between them.

'Shall we go inside? We can watch the lightning bounce off the sea if we're lucky.'

'If we're lucky?' Suddenly her teeth were chattering.

'It's spectacular.' His hands closed around her waist, and without effort he lifted her on to the poolside, and flipped himself easily out beside her. She registered with vague surprise that she was somehow becoming acclimatised to the unsettling feel of his hands on her body. . .

'Come on, we'll be safer inside, and dry. There's no need to look guilty about being frightened. Storms out here deserve a lot of respect.'

'*You're* frightened as well?' She found herself smiling at him suddenly as they gained the shelter of the sitting-room and went in search of towels. 'Brave man to admit it!'

He shot her an exasperated look, towelling his hair vigorously. 'If you watch how the lightning touches the water, you'll see the need for caution. I'm not exactly a gibbering wreck, am I?'

'No. . .' She couldn't help laughing now, towelling her

own hair and then wrapping the towel sarong-style while she crossed to the french doors.

There was no rain yet. But the storm was raging with almost primeval ferocity. Zigzags of white light split the blackness of the sky. As they watched, the lights in the villa suddenly failed. They were plunged into darkness, and the spectacle of the comets of white light arcing to the sea, and the ear-splitting crashed of thunder, became pure theatre.

'Am I exonerated from being a wimp?' Guy murmured, close to her ear.

'Mmm, I suppose so. . .'

With a husky laugh, he pulled her gently round to face him, and gave her a long, thorough appraisal, from the top of her head to the tip of her toes.

'You're looking better. You've gained a couple of pounds. And you've started to tan well. How are the headaches?'

'Going, I think. . .' Her voice didn't sound right. Too choked, too hoarse. She cleared her throat nervously. She ought to be furious at the patronising summary of her improved appearance. Instead, the feel of Guy's hands on her shoulders was ricocheting along every nerve-end in her body.

'You're trembling,' he said softly, the pale eyes darkening on her face. 'Are you cold?'

'No. . . I'm fine. . . Guy, don't. . .' Her voice dried, and she stared at him blankly, unsure what she'd been about to say.

'Don't what? Don't touch you? I've touched you several times tonight,' he teased softly. 'And you haven't hissed and scratched. Could it be you want me to touch you?'

'Guy. . .please. . .'

'Please what? Please don't kiss you?' It was breathed tauntingly close to her mouth. His breath was warm and fresh on her lips. 'It's a good thing you're such a chaste little man-hater, Virginia, because the trouble is I want to do a whole lot more than just kiss you. . .'

When he pulled her closer and slid his hands round her, she sucked in her breath involuntarily. He groaned softly as their bodies came together. He moulded his hands along the long, slender curve of her back, and the towel came untucked and slipped to the floor. The supple gold of her swimsuit felt as if it were melting under the heat generating between them.

'Guy, I feel. . . I don't know. . .' She wasn't making any sense. The warm ache had expanded and drowned out any reasoned responses. Letting her hands lift of their own volition, she slipped her fingers hungrily up the hard, stubble-roughened jawline and into the damp blackness of his hair.

His mouth found her parted lips with a sudden impatient roughness, and even in her drowning state of mindless arousal she thought she detected a flicker of surprise in his eyes as he felt her shudder against him. She shut her eyes then, letting this wanton fire creep through her. His tongue explored, then delved deeper. Sliding his hands up to her face, he cupped her head and thrust his tongue deeper still, as if he were dying of thirst, drinking from her.

Breaking apart, they stared at each other in stunned silence.

'For an uptight prude, you do a good line in sensual kissing,' he teased, breathing heavily.

'Maybe. . .maybe your character assessment is slightly flawed?' What was she *saying*.

In a detached way, as if she were somewhere else watching the scene unravel below, she saw Guy's eyes narrow and darken as his gaze moved assessingly over her.

'You're very beautiful, Virginia. . .' The words were rough, slightly uneven. Reaching out, he slid the straps of her swimsuit from her shoulders, then deliberately peeled the damp, clinging gold from her skin. The cooler night air touched her sensitised breasts before Guy's hands moved to explore their firm, upthrusting contours. When his fingers brushed lightly over the rigid nipples, she sank her teeth into her bottom lip in silent anguish. Guy bent his dark head, and stepped closer, let his lips and tongue caress where his fingers had been. Desire shook her to the very foundations of her being.

'Guy. . . I can hardly stand. . .' The agonised whisper brought his arms crushing round her, and she was hard against the heavy throb of his arousal, a thousand new sensations splintering through her. The coarse hair on his chest against her breasts was extraordinarily exciting.

'Let's lie down, then.' The throaty murmur triggered a surge of warmth inside her. 'I doubt if I can stay upright much longer.'

The big lattice-patterned bed in Guy's room brought back the moment when he'd marched in on her unannounced that first night. With the silky cover beneath her back, Virginia blinked up at the dark, muscular man above her. After the warm, sweet waves of fire a cooler, more panicky feeling was starting to invade her again. Words of warning were lurking somewhere in the darkest recesses of her mind, but the physical longing wasn't so easy to abruptly cancel out, and besides Guy was already peeling the rest of the gold swimsuit down to her waist, then straddling her to place strategic kisses along the path of exposed skin as he lifted her hips to ease the costume down to her thighs.

'You're delectable. . .' It was a groan of hunger, as she writhed in a sudden welter of dumb shyness as his lips and fingers sought intimate places which seemed to scream out to be covered up and left in decent privacy. . .

The back of her hand was pressed violently to her mouth, she dimly realised, and she was biting her knuckle so hard that she'd almost drawn blood. It was no good. The fear was still there. How did she relax and let herself trust again, after what Mortimer had done to her.

It was naïve to think she could hide her feelings from him. And if she'd imagined Guy Sterne as the kind of man who'd be sufficiently insensitive to ignore her panic, she was quickly proved wrong. Panic communicated itself silently. And Guy appeared to have no difficulty recognising it.

'Open your eyes, Virginia.' The command was soft but insistent. In the shadowy room, Guy loomed at her side, the black trunks stripped off, the taut, flat-muscled body naked. 'Look at me. . .'

Wide-eyed, her throat suddenly dry, she turned her head to stare at the length of his body.

'I want you. You can see how much I want you.' He dropped a long, searching kiss on her mouth, then took her shaking hand and laid it against the powerful, overpowering size of his arousal. 'But I'm not into rape and pillage of unwilling little girls. I want to make love *with* you. I don't want to be some substitute figure to feed your fantasies. . .'

'It's not that!' she whispered, horrified at his assumption. 'Really, it's not. . .'

'Well, whatever it is. . .' his voice was thick, unsteady with the depth of desire he was ruthlessly suppressing '. . .this stops right now. . .'

He levered himself away from her, as if he couldn't trust himself to stay close, swinging his feet to the floor and rubbing a distracted hand over his jaw, and up through his hair.

'I must need a brain scan,' he said finally, when the silence had hung endlessly. 'What the hell was I doing, trying to seduce Charles's little sister?'

'Don't make it sound so one-sided.' She spoke with tearful intensity, choking back tears. 'I'm sorry, Guy. It felt. . .it felt right. And. . .and then it felt all wrong again. . . I don't know how to explain. . .'

He turned round, his face in shadow.

'It's all right, Virginia,' he said quietly. 'You don't have to explain anything to me. Let's face it. . .' he reached to smooth back the curtain of tousled gold curls from her eyes '. . .we hardly know each other. Do we?'

His hand still shook slightly. Emotion welled up inside her, and with a strangled exclamation she turned her face into the pillow and wept, great shuddering sobs which hurt her chest.

'Virginia. . .' He'd moved closer again, reached to stroke the nape of her neck, but she violently shook him off.

'Don't touch me. Please!'

'OK. Calm down. Do you want to talk about it?'

Wordlessly, she shook her head. She hadn't a clue

what to say. He was right, anyway. They hardly knew each other. This ghastly episode must be the result of too much warm Caribbean sun, too much chilled Chardonnay and rum punch.

'I'm sorry, Guy. . .'

'Don't be sorry.' He stood up, disappeared to fetch her cotton wrap from her bedroom. 'Better to be safe,' he added wryly, handing her the flower-patterned gown. As if on cue, the lights flickered then came back on. She grabbed the wrap and hugged it round her, agonisingly aware of the swollen-eyed wreck she must look in the brightness. Guy looked blankly inscrutable, and supremely at ease with his own formidable nakedness.

'Thanks. . .' Mortified, she scrambled off the bed, and dashed for the door. 'Goodnight.'

'Goodnight, Virginia.' The thoughtful echo rang in her ears long after she'd buried herself beneath the bed cover in the privacy of her room, and yearned for the oblivion of sleep.

She ate breakfast alone on the terrace in the morning. When the minutes stretched by, and Guy still failed to appear, it was Tara who explained. Did she imagine the note of censure in the girl's soft voice?

'Guy has flown back to London. He had urgent business.'

'Oh. . .' It was impossible to hide her dismay. Guy had *gone*? Something akin to pain seared through her. Despite her confusion, she was achingly aware of a sharp sense of loss.

She tried to marshal her thoughts, but they skittered wildly. Had he gone back to Chester's? Would their sexual fiasco last night influence his attitudes to the company? Had he gone *because* of last night? Maybe he'd flown back to deal rapidly with Sarah Chester's, so that he was free of any embarrassing need to meet up with her again?

Or maybe he'd gone back to patch things up with his fiancée? Maybe that mystery phone call last night had been Nicola Schreider, or even Nicola's father, Guy's business partner? After all, they must have been engaged until relatively recently for Lucy to get her facts mixed up like that. . .

Humiliation began to creep through her. Presumably he must have arranged to fly back during that telephone call last night. The seduction scene afterwards must have been done with an eye for the main chance, before the opportunity disappeared. . .

She shut her eyes briefly, trying to make sense of her reactions. She might not trust Guy Sterne, she might not even like him very much, she might suspect him of being a ruthless womaniser and profiteer. . .but she *wanted* him here, *with* her. . .now where was the logic in that?

The cocoa-brown eyes were scanning her bewildered expression, and a glint of gentle amusement crept into the steady scrutiny.

'It was kind of a sudden decision. He asked me to tell you. Don't worry, I'll stay and look after the villa for you.'

'There's no need,' Virginia said quickly. 'In fact, I'd really rather cook and clean for myself, thanks, Tara. . .'

'Guy told me to stay on,' Tara said politely, taking the empty plate and cup from under her nose. 'He pays me to look after Hummingbird House.'

'Yes.' She glanced at the other girl's expression, trying to decipher her real meaning. 'I know. . .' She swallowed

on a suddenly dry throat. 'Is that all. . .? I mean, I've
sometimes got the impression that. . .that you and Guy
are, I mean. . .'

This was awful. Tara stared unblinkingly back at her.

'That Guy and I were lovers?' The girl nodded her
dark head slowly, a smile on her lips. 'Of course we
were, honey.' A small pink tongue outlined the full curve
of Tara's lips, and she laughed suddenly. 'Guy's a terrific
lover. He's the sort of man no girl in her right mind
would turn down, if you know what I mean. But he likes
variety. I've seen him looking at you. . .but he looks at
women that way. I'm lucky. He loves to relax. I can
help him relax. He loves Hummingbird House, and he
loves St Lucia. I'm here whenever he comes. So one day
soon, his next trip here, or the one after. . .maybe he'll
love me?'

'Yes. Maybe he will.'

Virginia felt as if a steel door had slammed shut inside
her. For the rest of her stay on the island, she didn't let
the ragged emotions of that near-miss encounter with
Guy trouble her mind for a single waking minute. She
swam and sunbathed, went sightseeing, worked on her
designs, talked brightly on the phone with Lucy, or Dad
or Charles whenever they rang her, forcing herself not to
ask whether Guy had moved in on the firm yet, and then
wincing when Lucy said that he'd made his mark in a
dramatic emergency board meeting, put up the backs of
most of the board of directors when he announced
sweeping measures to increase profitability, cut
overheads. . .

It was only at night, alone in bed, with the whirr of
the ceiling fan to keep her company, that the memory of

her crass stupidity swept back. She could only blame the sun, and the sea, and the insidious calypso music.

When she got back to England, and saw Guy Sterne in the cold, rain-soaked light of an English summer day, stability and common sense and some healthy, protective cynicism would undoubtedly reassert themselves without any effort on her part whatsoever.

CHAPTER SEVEN

'I MUST admit——' Charles picked at the end of his thumb and frowned out of the smoked glass office window at the leaden September sky beyond '—I'm not sure precisely what Guy's up to. Or what Dad's up to, for that matter. . .'

Virginia fixed him with a patient, expectant gaze across the desk, marvelling at her ability to stay calm and poised whenever the name of Guy Sterne entered the conversation these days. It was weeks since the night of thunder and lightning and losing her head in St Lucia. The fact that she hadn't seen Guy since made the episode in the Caribbean seem dreamlike—or nightmarish, she amended bitterly.

'Dad's playing ostrich. I should know—playing ostrich is a habit I've inherited from him! But Guy Sterne's playing power games, Charles. I don't understand why you can't *see* that!'

'Virgie, Guy's an old friend of mine——'

'And all's fair in friendship and business!'

Charles flicked back the lock of straight brown hair which habitually fell into his eyes, and shrugged with a touch of irritation.

'Virgie, listen to me. Dad may be playing ostrich, but you're clucking round the family business like a jealous hen——'

'I am *not*! How do *you* feel about Dad appointing Guy managing director? Surely you must have some urge to

110

fight for the company Gran founded on caring, sharing principles. . .?'

'Without Guy Sterne, the bank didn't want to know. Now they're extending our line of credit. They're happy to back a complete new product line. Guy's come up with this patent for a new system from America which cuts turn-around time in the garment-sewing factories by some amazing percentage and——'

'Fine. It all sounds fine,' Virginia cut in quietly, green eyes flashing with the intensity of her feelings. 'But if you know all this, why can't *you* mastermind everything? Why do we have to bring in a cut-throat operator like Guy Sterne?'

Charles pulled a wry face. 'You're forgetting the bank. In their eyes, the Chesters have had plenty of time to come up with solutions, and lacked the initiative. They've got confidence in Guy. They haven't got confidence in the old board of directors, and that includes me, and Dad——'

'All right. . .if Guy is so committed to Sarah Chester Fabrics' resurrection, *why* is he never here? Why is everything cloak and dagger?'

Charles shot her a bleak, hunted look. 'That's just the way Guy's always operated.'

'So the saviour and the executioner both act the same way?'

'Who's being executed?'

The clipped drawl from the doorway made Virginia turn slowly, heart sinking. She'd know his voice anywhere, she realised furiously—in dense fog and darkness, at the furthest ends of the earth. She tensed up immediately at the prospect of seeing him again, but when she turned right round her heart flipped idiotically in her

chest. Gone was the relaxed, taunting, casually dressed
man of Hummingbird House and St Lucia. In dark
City-striped suit, dark silk tie, ice-white shirt contrasting
sharply with his hard, tanned face, Guy Sterne looked a
formidable adversary. He looked like a stranger.

'Hello, Guy.' Charles was all welcoming smiles,
'You've just missed a board meeting, old man. How's it
all going?'

The grey-green gaze briefly acknowledged Charles,
but concentrated intently on Virginia. From a state of
poise and self-confidence, she was suddenly overwhelmingly self-conscious. In an instant she was aware of every
detail of her appearance from the upswept Titian curls,
tamed for the meeting that had just broken up in
fragmented dissatisfaction among the main body of the
directors, to her neat cinnamon gabardine suit and
matching high court shoes. She ran her tongue nervously
over her lips, tasting the honey-coral lipgloss she'd
applied carefully in an effort to banish her image as the
ingenuous young art student, fresh from college.

'Hello, Virginia. You're looking very. . .grown-up.'

She wanted to snap, I *am* very grown-up, but decided
this would negate the claim. She forced a polite smile
instead.

'Thanks. So are you.'

The quip failed to provoke a smile.

'Sorry to miss the meeting, Charles. I've been having
lunch with the chairman of Farthingdales.'

'They're our biggest competitor,' Virginia pointed out,
unnecessarily. She won a gleam of mocking agreement
from Guy.

'Well spotted. It's interesting to find out what the
opposition's up to.'

'More interesting than sharing your schemes and plans with the board of Chester's, I expect.'

'Absolutely.'

There was a short, charged pause. Charles chewed the tip of his thumb, then jumped as the telephone on his desk shrilled loudly.

'Problems over in brand management.' He smiled at them briefly, replacing the receiver and standing up, 'Duty calls. See you later, Guy.'

With a casual lift of his hand, Charles had gone, leaving Virginia to face Guy across the empty office. The atmosphere grew warier.

'How are you, Virginia?' Guy broke the silence at last, the pale gaze intent on her flushed face. 'You look well.'

'A suntan does help, doesn't it? Actually, I'm feeling well,' she managed to retort coolly, succeeding after an immense effort to blot out the powerful sensual images of their last night in St Lucia. 'After you'd gone, I didn't do much apart from swim, sunbathe and sleep.'

'I had a feeling you'd make a better recovery without me around.' There was no intonation in the remark. The unemotional gaze remained steady on her face.

'I hope you didn't cut short your holiday for that reason?'

He shook his head slowly. 'I'm not quite that altruistic.' He glanced at his watch. 'I have to go. There's someone I have to see. I'll see you tonight?'

Her frozen surprise made him pause at the door, a gleam of amusement touching his eyes for the first time.

'Your father didn't tell you?'

'Tell me *what*?'

'He's offered me a room at Armscott whenever I'm down in Oxfordshire.' The wide mouth twisted at her appalled expression. 'I understand your Mrs Chalk is cooking pheasant in red wine tonight. Seven-thirty for eight. See you for pre-dinner drinks.'

With a nod he'd gone, closing the door quietly behind him.

Driving back to Armscott Manor, Virginia felt as if a small bomb had been detonated in her life. What on earth was Dad thinking of? Maybe he was suffering from premature senile dementia? Armscott Manor was vast and rambling, admittedly. But it was their *home*. . .inviting Guy Sterne to use it as a convenient guest-house was like flinging open the drawbridge to the enemy. . .

Parking the Volvo under the cedar tree, she was so sunk in her own angry thoughts that she hardly felt the bleak rain on her face as she walked slowly round to the rear entrance. It had been a terrible summer, she reflected, one of those damp, chilly English summers which could almost be mistaken for one of their recent damp, mild winters. The gardens were a sea of dripping green, the roses and late-flowering sweet-peas water-logged.

Dad knew how she felt in general about Guy. But he couldn't know her personal feelings for him. She hung her wet Burberry on a peg in the lobby, and glanced into various downstairs rooms to see if her father was around. She could attempt to talk to him, try to make sense of what was going on. But he was nowhere to be seen.

Mrs Chalk was clattering round in the kitchen, and a savoury aroma was wafting from that region. She'd go and offer to help, when she'd changed and popped in to see Lucy. . .

'He's only going to sleep in one of the numerous empty guest rooms, Virgie, love!' Lucy remonstrated, when Virginia had made them both a cup of tea and perched herself on the edge of Lucy's bed. Her sister-in-law looked deceptively healthy and serene, propped against the pillows. It was difficult to believe the doctor's warning, but they were all taking Lucy's ante-natal relaxation very seriously, Lucy included. She spent each afternoon in bed, coming down for dinner and then lying on the sofa afterwards. The alternative was hospitalisation until the baby was born, and Dr Newne was prone to making unannounced visits to satisfy himself that his orders were being followed to the letter. 'You'll hardly even notice he's around. According to Charles he's mostly in London, anyway!'

'I gathered that. Pronouncing sentence from afar.'

'Besides, Armscott's always had room for everyone! Look how well Charles and I fit into our own quarter of it!'

'But why am I always the last to know?'

Lucy grinned. 'I imagine Dad knew how you'd react to having Guy at Armscott. You know how he hates scenes! By the way, have you heard the rumours about Nicola Schreider?'

'Do I want to?'

'She and Guy have split up. I'll bet that's made for a few tensions in Schreider Sterne Inc.!'

Serve him right, Virginia thought uncharitably, but some buried corner of her rejoiced that Guy had told the truth, at least on that score. . . She despised the treacherous reaction, smothered it immediately.

Lucy was eyeing her changing expression speculatively.

'You've been very quiet and cagey since you got back from St Lucia. I'm *itching* to know how you and Guy got on. He's such good company. I refuse to believe you didn't thaw.'

Virginia was mortified to find colour creeping into her face.

'That depends how you mean "thaw",' she conceded coolly, 'Frankly I wouldn't trust him one inch. But I'll admit he's quite fun to be with.'

That much was true, she acknowledged reluctantly, taking a gulp of tea to hide from Lucy's probing eyes. Abruptly, it dawned on her that what had hurt most that fateful night of the storm was Guy's detached dismissal of any real rapport between them. He'd cut short her agonised attempts to blurt out her problems. 'We hardly know each other.' That was what he'd said.

Virginia closed her eyes for a second, fighting this odious revelation. How could she be so pathetically mixed-up? How could she detest him, despise him, distrust him, and at the same time crave his friendship? After only a couple of days, comprising mainly insults and bickering, she hadn't *felt* as if they were strangers. She'd felt as if she'd been fighting with Guy Sterne all her life! It didn't make any sense. Nothing seemed to any more.

'Hey, cheer up,' Lucy urged softly, and Virginia opened her eyes guiltily, with a hasty smile. 'How was the girlfriend in St Lucia? Tara, was that her name?'

'Oh, she's crazy about him. But I got the impression he was just using her.' Just as he would have been using Nicola Schreider, she reflected with sudden cold certainty. She had her thoughts under control again, thank heavens. With a flash of insight, she imagined Guy's jilted fiancée had received a timely escape. He might be amazingly good to look at, he might be brilliant company, he might possibly be an amazing lover, though she couldn't truthfully testify to that in depth, but jokes and. . .and *sex* weren't everything. Nicola Schreider would surely come to relish her freedom from the agonising uncertainty of loving Guy Sterne. . .

Loving Guy Sterne? Her throat had gone dry. It took an enormous effort to drag her thoughts on to safer ground.

'Frankly, Nicola Schreider needs a shrink if she doesn't put up a good fight for him. Guy's just about the most irresistible male I've ever set eyes on,' Lucy said dreamily, adding hastily, 'Next to Charles, of course!'

But it was Guy Lucy sat next to at dinner. Pregnancy had lent a translucent quality to her looks, but the smiles she frequently aimed at Guy seemed to contain an extra radiance. Guy's spare, witty style of conversation lifted what would have been a family dinner into a special occasion. And there was a small surprise in store. A bottle of vintage champagne was cracked open, and a toast drunk to Virginia's exam results received a few days earlier. Her father's expression was the warmest she'd seen it for a long time.

The tired green eyes were crinkled in a smile, his voice rueful. 'I've a sneaky feeling you think I haven't taken you seriously enough, over the years. But I'm very proud of you, and your mother would have been, too. . .you worked harder than most to get that degree, my dear, even putting your health at risk. . .' She felt her throat tighten as they kissed cheeks and sipped the effervescent chill of the Veuve Cliquot. 'So here's to your full recovery, and a brilliant future, Ginny, darling.'

'Thanks, Dad. . .' She gave him a quick, hard hug. The brief look they exchanged seemed to heal numerous unspoken resentments. Her eyes were prickling with ridiculous tears when they all settled back down to eat. With a furious blink, she met Guy's intent appraisal across the table, and whipped her gaze away as if she'd been burned. To cover her confusion she enquired after the latest entertaining village gossip from Lucy, who was prone to whiling away hours at the ante-natal clinic in deep conversation with fellow village wives. Amused speculation on whether the new vicar could really be casting lustful glances at the choir-mistress produced an effective antidote to the emotional tension a few minutes earlier.

Talk and laughter flowed easily around the table from then on, though business wasn't discussed. Her father recounted his latest golf tournament, Guy talked to Charles about sailing, then opened up the conversation by introducing a surprisingly shrewd appreciation of the arts into the debate, when it became clear that in addition to racing yachts around the Isle of Wight he made frequent visits to see the RSC at the Barbican, and was something of an expert on modern ballet.

It was on the tip of her tongue to pour scorn and disbelief on the idea of Guy liking ballet. Ballet definitely didn't jell with the image of super-macho, cool-as-ice City slicker. Then she recalled his reactions to what he'd labelled her prejudices in St Lucia, and stayed silent.

Another image came to mind, strangely tormenting. A vision of Tara's sleek dancer's body, closely followed by Guy's muscular suppleness during that limbo contest. Maybe ballet wasn't such an unlikely taste to contemplate. . .absently pleating the soft floral skirt of her summer dress between her fingers, she firmly resisted the temptation to mock.

'About Sarah Chester's. . .' Maybe it was the abrupt pain of thinking about Tara, or the sudden recollection that this man blending so effortlessly into the family gathering was not to be trusted, but Virginia found herself cutting into the convivial mood and causing a sudden, rather surprised silence.

'Can we all talk about the future of the family business, or is that some taboo subject never to be discussed at mealtimes?' She glanced around the varying expressions, and focussed finally on Guy's calm, unreadable gaze. In ice-grey and white striped shirt and charcoal cord trousers, there was a cool, ruthless elegance in every muscular angle of his body. Did she imagine the slight hardening of his expression? She swallowed hard, waiting for someone to respond. But no one seemed in any hurry to do so.

Her father and Charles appeared deeply preoccupied in finishing their pheasant, and Lucy just looked acutely embarrassed.

'Well?' she persisted recklessly. 'Since we've got our captive financial expert at our mercy tonight, and since we so rarely have the pleasure of seeing him, shouldn't we demand a progress report?'

She gave Guy a sleek smile to underline her words. 'I don't even work at Chester's, but I know a lot of the management are unhappy. They think you're fattening the company up for slaughter. . .what *exactly* are you planning for Chester's, Guy?'

'Virginia, for heaven's sake. . .' Charles's low plea was interrupted by Guy, who was slowly turning the stem of the cut-glass wine goblet in front of him, watching the reflection of candlelight in the dark burgundy.

'I have several projects for the future of Sarah Chester's,' he countered softly. 'But I'm not in a position to discuss them right now.'

He was being deliberately evasive, Virginia thought angrily. And that could only mean one thing.

'You can't fob us off like this for long——' she began heatedly.

'Ginny, I've made Guy MD of Chester's on good advice. . .' Her father raked agitated fingers through his grey hair. 'And frankly, darling, your degree is in textile design, not business and finance. You don't know what you're talking about——'

'The future of Chester's is a dicey area to predict,' Guy went on coldly, the clipped flatness of his voice deterring further interruption. 'The impossible might be achieved overnight. Miracles may take a little longer. But the company's past and present I can sum up quite quickly, if you like. Unless the bank see new management, Virginia, the company your grandparents established is rapidly going to go down the pan——'

'But the fire caused this crisis——'

'The fire just highlighted a problem that was already there. And incidentally the new singeing machine didn't catch fire on its own. That was operator error. The gas was turned too high. A symptom of a company which has expanded too fast in terms of expensive machinery, clung to its principles of manufacturing, storing, distributing and retailing entirely through its own central management, without expanding its product lines or investing in sufficient skilled training. You've opened dozens of new Sarah Chester high street outlets, but you're losing your market. Your product range passed its peak quite a while ago, and no one noticed. You need radical change in tactics, and investment, to survive. I'm the bank's security on investment.'

The unemotional summary was over. Virginia, white-faced, stared at the flickering gold candles in the central silver candelabra, unsure what to say. She'd asked for a terse put-down, she reflected with some justice. Guy had proved himself a past master at the art.

Why had she opened her big mouth? What had she hoped to achieve? A man like Guy Sterne wasn't likely to blurt out a confession of guilt at the first accusation, was he? Besides, what he said seemed, on the surface, to make sense. She didn't trust him, but without solid evidence she had no way of proving he was double-dealing.

The worst thing was, his response had reduced her to feeling like a chastened schoolgirl, a feeling she'd hoped she'd outgrown.

'Thank you, Guy,' her father cut in quietly, rose-tinted blinkers clearly firmly in place. 'Now, shall we have some pudding? Let me see if I can guess which one you made, Virginia? The baked raisin cheesecake?'

'Correct.' She gave him a thin smile, battling with her resentment. 'Are you going to try some?'

'Definitely. I can recommend it, Guy,' he added, glancing over at their guest. 'And how's the job-hunting going, darling?'

'Oh. . .fine.' She took a deep breath, made the effort to be mature enough to pick up the olive branch. 'I've applied to every heavyweight interior design company I can think of. The thing is, if I'm going to start my own business one day, I want to get good experience working for the best. . .so I don't care whether I'm answering the phone or working in their library. As long as I'm there, an opportunity will come up. . .'

'Have you had any response so far?'

'No. . .but I'm going up to Olympia tomorrow. Everyone who's anyone should be there. . .'

'The fashion and textile exhibition?' Lucy queried, on a half-yawn. Her eyes were drooping. An ability to fall asleep any time, anywhere had been a feature of Lucy's pregnancy right from the start.

'Yes. I'll go armed with a few of my best designs, just in case my big break awaits me!'

'Take a look at Chester's stand, while you're there,' Charles suggested with a wry grin.

'As if I wouldn't——'

'If you're up in London tomorrow——' Guy broke into the conversation calmly, having opted for a wedge of Virginia's baked raisin cheesecake in preference to fresh strawberries, or rich chocolate gâteau, 'I've got two tickets for the American Ballet Theatre.' He raised a cool eyebrow at Virginia as she spooned a strawberry into her mouth. 'Tomorrow night, at the Coliseum. Would you like to come with me?'

'Virginia adores Ballet Rambert,' Lucy put in helpfully, ignoring the fiercely repressive look she received in return.

'Thanks all the same, but I'm going to be busy tomorrow night. . .' she began coldly, putting her spoon back into her dish with a clumsy clatter which splashed strawberry and sugar juice on to her lap. She stared unseeingly down at the red stain on the Chester's blue and green flowered fabric, then gathered her wits to dab at it slowly with her heavy cream damask napkin she took from the table.

'Are you staying up in town overnight?' Lucy wanted to know.

'I may do. Some of my art school friends will be at Olympia. Remember Kit and Teresa?' Virginia spoke quickly, lightly, avoiding Guy's eyes. 'Some of their degree collections are going to be featured in a catwalk show. They're hoping one of the big fashion houses might buy them. . .'

Charles whistled slowly. 'Setting their sights high, aren't they?'

Virginia shrugged, standing up. The stain needed soaking. It was a good excuse to make her escape. . .

'We're all setting our sights high,' she countered simply. 'Why not?'

'Why not indeed?' Guy murmured softly. She ignored him, hardly daring to meet his penetrating gaze.

'I'll go and sponge this strawberry juice off my dress, if you'll all excuse me? Then I think I might grab an early night. . .'

She bent quickly to kiss her father, then let herself out into the shadowy hall, and made for the wide, oak-panelled stairs. It was rude and rather self-indulgent, she reflected guiltily, dashing off to bed like this. Stacking the dishwasher frequently proved a puzzle to Mrs Chalk, and Virginia usually helped with the clearing away after meals. . .

'Virginia, wait. . .'

She'd made it to her bedroom door before Guy's voice called after her.

'Hey, slow down. . .' The wide, centuries-old oak floorboards on the landing creaked softly as Guy reached the top of the stairs and caught up with her. There was a grimly humorous light in his eyes. 'What's the hurry?'

'I need to get this dress off and in soak. . .' she began stiffly, then caught his sardonic expression and blushed angrily. The soft pink and green striped duvet-cover on her bed was visible through the open door of her bedroom. She was physically aware of Guy's nearness, she admitted, in every cell of her body. The knowledge made her rigid with self-consciousness.

'Don't look so alarmed,' he advised quietly. 'I learned my lessons in St Lucia, Virginia. I'm not offering to help you take your dress off.' His eyes roved mockingly over the tanned curve of her breasts at the unbuttoned neckline of the dress as he spoke, and she shivered despairingly.

She glared at him. Of course he wasn't, an inner voice taunted. She'd really humiliated herself, that night in St Lucia. . .damn Guy Sterne to hell. She'd thrown herself at him, and then when she'd panicked he'd dropped her like a hot potato. . .what a fool she'd been! He'd wanted casual sex, not a counselling session. But what had *she* wanted? Here I go again, she thought desperately, chasing round in mental circles. . .

'Why did you follow me up here?' Her hands had gone, involuntarily, to the buttons on her bodice, her fingers defensively closing the gap.

'Those designs you did in St Lucia,' he said finally, his tone thoughtful. 'I'd rather you didn't tout those around Chester's competitors at Olympia tomorrow. . .'

'*What*. . .?' She wondered at first if she'd heard him right. In stunned amazement, she stared at him.

'What on earth do you mean?' she demanded angrily, gathering her wits. 'Guy, my name may be Chester, but

I am not an employee of Sarah Chester Fabrics. You can't give me orders. They're my designs, I'll do what the hell I like with them——'

'I'm interested in them. Chester's need a new product line. I've done some intensive market research. After a summer like this, I believe those subtle, tropical-style patterns of yours could be just what we need. I'd like to discuss some ideas with you. . .'

Her eyes widened involuntarily on his bland, unreadable expression. Her brain was reeling. This was so unexpected. . .the very *last* thing she'd have expected from Guy Sterne. . .

'Is this some kind of joke?'

'No joke. Trust me, Virginia.' The deep drawl was impossible to decipher.

She shook her head slowly. He had to have an ulterior motive. Common sense told her so. But what? What possible reason could he have for trying to convince her that *her* designs could help save Chester's?

'I suppose I should be bowled over? Terribly flattered?' she said at last, in a voice not quite like her own. 'But frankly, you're not a design consultant. . .'

'That doesn't mean I can't recognise a good design when I see it.'

She put a hand to her forehead, frowning fiercely up at him. 'So. . .what are you saying, exactly? I mean. . .people who only succeed through their family connections depress me,' she went on frantically, her head spinning at the glittering lures being dangled before her eyes. 'I haven't worked for my degree just to be handed a cosy role in the family firm! I'm keen to make my mark on my own merits, not because I happen to be the chairman's daughter!'

'I'm the managing director,' he pointed out evenly, 'You're not my daughter. I'd like to appoint you to Chester's design team. As for a cosy role in the family firm, forget it. There's nothing cosy about a firm that's about to sink without trace!'

'I'm sorry. . . I can't believe you genuinely think that. . .that *my* little designs in St Lucia would make any difference to the hundreds of pattern designs used by Sarah Chester Fabrics. . .'

'What was that remark about setting your sights high?' he queried sardonically.

'That's *different*!' she burst out frustratedly. 'Surely you can see that?'

'How is it different?' Guy shrugged with a sudden, impatient anger. 'You're a talented designer, Virginia. You have enough confidence in your abilities to talk of your own interior design business. Now you're dismissing your own work as inadequate?'

There was a charged silence.

'There may be some unpleasant changes in store for Chester's. I want to recommend some positive changes to soften the blow. I want a fresh range of designs, linked with a totally new concept,' Guy went on evenly. 'I had in mind a "mother and child" range. Co-ordinating clothes, styles, soft furnishings, with a mother and child theme. I think it would work.'

Virginia chewed her lip reflectively, her mind in turmoil.

'Sounds sexist to me,' she commented finally, her voice cool. 'What about the fathers?'

'I'm open to suggestions.' Guy's gaze held a glitter of grim amusement at last. 'Well? What do you say? Are you going to sacrifice the chance to help Chester's on the altar of your pride and independence, Virginia?'

'That's not fair! I just don't know——'

'Think it over,' he said abruptly. 'Let me know your decision.'

He turned and walked away, leaving her standing by the open door of her bedroom, staring after him in an agony of confusion.

She had plenty of time to think it over during a sleepless night, and on the train in the morning. In fact, the whole vexed question of Guy Sterne, her mixed-up feelings about him, and his true motives for offering her the design job, occupied her mind throughout her journey. Staring out of the carriage window at the dismal, wind-torn countryside, a plastic cup of weak British Rail coffee untouched in front of her, she brooded non-stop all the way to London.

It's no joke, he'd said. Trust me. Well, that was a joke in itself. Every instinct told her she'd be naïve to trust him.

She crossed one suede-booted leg over the other, and toyed with the belt of her Burberry, her green eyes unfocused on the passing scenery. The middle-aged businessman opposite lifted his eyes from a sheaf of papers in his briefcase and stared with fixed interest at the soft-faced girl with the golden tan and the riot of Titian curls, but Virginia was supremely unaware of his admiration. What if Guy was really trying to help Chester's? If he genuinely felt her designs could form the basis for a new range to lift the company's fortunes? Could she pursue her cherished independence, if Chester's *really* needed her?

She felt illogically furious with Guy for putting her in such an impossible position. Maybe it was deliberate. A subtle form of blackmail? She debated the likelihood of this as she strolled around the crowded exhibition at Olympia, too preoccupied to take in much of her surroundings. Did he just get a kick out of being in control, and saw this as a clever way of controlling her, as well as Sarah Chester Fabrics?

She was making her way to the Chester's stand, sunk in thought, when the familiar sandy-haired man loomed in front of her. She nearly collided with him.

'Ginny! Sweetheart! What luck, bumping into you here! Literally bumping into you!' He laughed, without real humour.

She stared at him unsmilingly, a sick feeling in her stomach. 'Hello, Mortimer.'

'How are you, Ginny?'

'Fine. . .excuse me. . .' She made to pass him, but he grasped her arm, detaining her.

'Congratulations on your degree. I knew you'd get a first. You were always my star student. . . Don't rush off. If you knew how I've longed to see you again, sweetheart——'

'I am not your sweetheart; I never was!' she informed him, through clenched teeth. 'Get out of my way, Mortimer——'

'Ginny, be sensible, darling. Come and have a drink with me. We can't talk here. . .' Perspiration was beading the fair, freckled skin of his forehead. There were wet rings of sweat marking the top of his shirt-sleeves under his arms. Suddenly she felt physically ill, consumed with violent panic. . .

'We can't talk anywhere. Get out of my way, leave me alone!'

Fear lifted her voice to a higher pitch, and one or two people around them glanced curiously in their direction.

'You're being hysterical, Ginny. . .' She couldn't seem to wrench her eyes from the heated blue gaze devouring her. He was using his soft, reasonable tone now, his professional lecturer tone he'd always switched to when he wanted to wield authority. 'I left Margaret for you. You owe me for that!'

'Go to hell, Mortimer,' she said with intense distaste. 'You're sick. You need *treatment*. . .'

They were silently wrestling now, in the middle of the crowded exhibition hall, and it wasn't until a clipped, flat drawl spoke behind her that Mortimer's vice-like grip was abruptly released from her wrists.

'What's going on here, Virginia?'

'Guy!' The sudden freedom from Mortimer's grip made her stagger slightly, and she grasped Guy's arm to steady herself, trembling all over with reaction. The flood of gratitude she felt at Guy's surprise appearance was as illogically powerful as the tide of resentment she'd been harbouring earlier.

'Who the devil are you?' Mortimer was eyeing Guy with belligerence, but his querulous challenge lacked conviction. His bullying tactics had always been reserved for the weaker sex, Virginia guessed bitterly. Guy topped Mortimer's height by at least six inches, and the civilising garb of Savile Row suit and Jermyn Street silk shirt did nothing to hide his athletic physique.

'Virginia's. . .friend,' Guy countered softly. His gaze was very hard, and there was an ominously grim violence in his voice. 'A status you clearly lack. So unless you come up with a bloody good reason why you're assaulting Virginia in broad daylight in the middle of a London exhibition I strongly advise you to get the hell out of here. Now!'

CHAPTER EIGHT

'Do YOU want to tell me about it?'

She was sitting in the relative sanctuary of Guy's iron-grey Aston Martin as they negotiated heavy traffic across London. He'd taken one look at her ashen face, and steered her out of the swirling throngs of people without needing to be asked.

'Who was that man, Virginia?' he persisted quietly, as they waited at more traffic lights.

'One of my course tutors at college.'

'Does he still teach there?'

She shook her head miserably, biting back the urge to howl like a baby.

'Just as well. Or I'd make sure he didn't for much longer.'

'Guy, please. . .' She flung out her hand involuntarily to touch his arm, then stopped, unsure of herself. 'Don't. . .interfere. It's over. Finished. I don't want anything raked up.'

The chiselled line of Guy's jaw looked even tighter, but he said nothing else until they reached his Docklands flat. There she found herself ensconced in a huge grey suede and chrome armchair, clutching a hefty measure of Scotch, and staring blankly around at what she could only assume to be the 'minimalist' style of interior decoration. With huge plate glass windows overloooking the pewter-grey Thames below, and the dove-grey sky above, the monochrome scheme in the flat was decidedly unnerving, she decided.

'Feeling better?'

She sipped the fiery spirit, and blinked. 'I'm not sure. . .this flat is hideous, Guy!'

'Isn't it?' he agreed blandly. 'I must have been feeling manic depressive when I had this done. It's due for redecoration.'

'Did you choose the colour scheme?'

'Guilty.'

'What about Hummingbird House? Did you choose the colours for that too?' she queried, bewildered. He nodded, putting down his drink on a black marble table and coming over to take hers from her numb fingers.

'Yes. I picked the colour schemes for Hummingbird House too,' he agreed gently, overwhelming her with his nearness as he crouched in front of her. 'I've got this irksome fetish for using the natural colours surrounding a place to decorate the interior—but I didn't bring you here to discuss my schizophrenic choice of living surroundings, Virginia. Tell me about the man at the exhibition.'

'Guy. . .' She stopped, suddenly drowning in a confused, illogical longing to confide in this man, and wishing with all her heart that she wasn't so terrified of the consequences. 'Oh, Guy. . .'

'Tell me. I need to know.' The grey-green eyes were very intent on the shadowy uncertainty in hers. He straightened up and pulled another chair closer, sitting opposite her in an attitude of relaxed attention. 'If he's the reason you're afraid of sex I'd like to hear about it.'

'Why?' The challenge came out hoarsely.

'Because for some extremely tiresome reason I've discovered I care about you.'

The colour flooded her face, then receded, leaving her paler than ever beneath the surface tan.

'What does that mean?' she whispered unevenly, unable to take her eyes off the dark, angular face opposite her. 'That you're keen to finish what you started in St Lucia, so you'd like to rid me of my inconvenient hang-ups?'

'No.' His eyes hardened. 'It means that when I'm with you I find it annoyingly hard to think straight. When I see you I get a clenched feeling in the gut as though I've been punched. When I'm not with you I find myself thinking about you all the bloody time.'

She clenched her hands into small fists at her sides, then unclenched them again. Her throat felt so dry that she wasn't sure if her voice would work properly.

'Is that supposed to sound romantic?'

'It's supposed to sound honest.' With a sudden abrupt tug, he loosened his tie, and raked his hand through his dark hair.

'Does. . .does the invitation to the ballet still stand?'

'To hell with the bloody ballet? Virginia, for the love of God, will you just talk to me? Tell me what's happened to you?'

She shrugged stiffly, aware that her heart was thudding against her breastbone with uncomfortable speed.

'The man at the exhibition was Mortimer Harrison. He. . .he tried to rape me once. . .'

She stopped. Once the words were out, she was appalled by how raw and painful and sordid they sounded. She felt as if she'd uncovered a dark pit of long-buried feelings, and she was terrified of peering too far inside in case she couldn't cope with the contents. . .

Guy's eyes darkened, but his expression didn't alter. 'Go on,' he prompted, his voice dangerously quiet.

'He was. . .oh, lord, I don't know. . .infatuated with me? It started as a friendship. He was one of my tutors, I respected his views, that kind of thing. He was a keen rambler. We. . .we used to go on rambling weekends, with a group of ramblers. It was a club. . .'

She dried up again, and reached to take a sip of her whisky. It was only then she realised she was shivering. The amber liquid shook in the glass and some of it spilled on to the tan cloth of her Burberry. Guy stood up abruptly and took the glass from her nerveless fingers, drawing her up and pulling her very gently into his arms.

The warmth from him seemed to envelop her, like the comforting heat of the sun. With a smothered exclamation, she rested her face against the smooth material of his dark suit jacket. The tears came, and wouldn't stop.

'It's all right. . .it doesn't matter. . .' The husky words were said into her hair.

'I'm sorry. . .you'll have mascara on your shirt. . .'

'To hell with the shirt.'

'It was awful, Guy,' she whispered, after a long time when neither of them moved or spoke.

'It's all right. Just tell me about it. . .'

'He. . .he made it seem as if it was somehow. . .*my* fault. Something I'd done. . .' She stopped again, struggling with the torrent of emotions she'd unleashed. 'And sometimes I've wondered if it *was* my fault. . .after my mother died I felt so lost, it was as if I needed someone to fill the void she left. This sounds silly, but that's how it felt. Mortimer seemed to be so supportive, he seemed really interested in me as a friend, he believed in my design abilities. . .but then it all changed, it was like a nightmare. I swear I never, ever saw him as anything but my tutor, and a fellow rambler and a friend. But he came round to my digs one night, when my friends were out. . .without any warning. . .he just went mad. If Kit and Teresa hadn't come back when they did. . .'

She shuddered convulsively, and Guy's arms tightened round her. He stroked her hair with one hand.

'Unless you want this man strangled, don't give me his address,' he muttered harshly.

'I don't know where he lives. He was married, you see, but he told me today he'd left his wife. For me! It makes me feel ill to think of that. . .'

'He can't have been much fun to live with; his wife wouldn't necessarily have been heartbroken,' Guy commented drily, finally releasing her and going in search of a large box of tissues. 'Did you tell the police what happened?'

'No!' She scrubbed her swollen face with a three-ply tissue, and blew her nose. 'In fact. . .' she swallowed, realisation dawning on her as she met Guy's intent appraisal '. . .you're the first person I've told. . .'

There was a silence. Guy's eyes were very brilliant when she risked looking at him. The atmosphere between them seemed to vibrate with some invisible electricity.

'So. . .your friends Kit and Teresa came back to your digs before he'd technically raped you?'

'Yes.'

'But they must have realised something had been going on?'

'They. . .' She caught her breath, and Guy reached out and took her hand between both of his. 'I think they thought Mortimer and I were having an affair,' she finished up bitterly. 'But I was terrified to tell anyone what had really happened—he was quite capable of deliberately sabotaging my degree work if I did. Besides, the next day I went down with glandular fever. I was really ill for a few weeks. I went home for half-term. And when I got back for the last few weeks Mortimer had left. . .'

'Was he sacked?'

'I presume so. . .but I don't know. Some of the other staff might have noticed his obsession with me. I really don't know. That's the worst part about it. But he's still involved in the design industry—or he wouldn't have been at the Olympia exhibition, would he?'

Her sudden fresh fear communicated itself, and with a muttered obscenity Guy pulled her back into his arms.

'Forget him. Do you hear me, Virginia? Forget the bastard.'

The gentle, rhythmical stroke of his hands on her back was soothing, but she was still shivering.

'Sometimes I've thought I'll never forget what happened. . .it all comes back and I feel guilty, or. . .or dirty, or humiliated and bitter. . . Forgetting is not so easy. . .'

Guy tilted her chin up to face him, and lowered his mouth gently to cover her parted lips, and she was quite ridiculously unprepared for the surge of resonating need, swamping her senses.

'I'd like to make it easy. . .' It was breathed against

her lips, as they came up for air, and the erotic fire scorching through her made her dizzy with illicit longing. Head spinning, she clung to him, shuddering with emotion. It was Guy who halted the spiral of desire. With a deep, shaky breath he thrust them apart, and swept his eyes the length of her body, with the eyes of a starving man denying himself food.

'Jeez!' he hissed softly. 'What the hell do I do with you?'

'Put me on the next train home?' she suggested unsteadily, her pulses skittering recklessly. How could it be that this one man made her feel like this? What sort of chemistry turned you off so totally with most people, but lit a hectic bonfire inside you with one special person?

'I wish I could be that noble.'

He still held them apart, at a bearable distance, a pulse in his cheek betraying his feelings. Distant notes of caution crept into her thoughts, instantly swamped by the horde of frightening, exciting feelings teeming around inside her. But they were still there, she realised, all those doubts. . .nothing had changed, just because she happened to have ricocheted from Mortimer's clutches into Guy's arms this afternoon, just because Guy Sterne's physical chemistry created a minor explosion when it mingled with hers. . .

But his duplicity over Tara seemed a distant, minor consideration. But what about his honesty over Sarah Chester Fabrics. . .his treatment of his fiancée Nicola. . .his entire reputation as a self-interested entrepreneur with a flexible approach to integrity. . .? Did this *have* to be the person she entrusted with her fragile emotions?

'I just happen to have two tickets to the American Ballet Theatre tonight,' Guy said, reflectively. 'Would you like to come, Virginia?' The dry note of humour lightened the growing tension.

'I've a feeling it would finish rather late. . .' she began uncertainly. 'I'm not sure when the last train goes. . .'

'You *could* spend the night here, with me?'

Colour surged and receded in her face. 'Guy. . .' She felt as if the breath had been suddenly knocked out of her. 'Guy. . . I'm not sure I. . .'

'You were quite safe in St Lucia,' he reminded her softly. 'You'll be safe in my spare room here.'

He saw the flicker of doubt in her eyes, and added with a husky laugh, 'I'm not saying I don't want you. I'm no saint. I'm no pervert, either, Virginia. I like my women willing and eager. . .'

She blinked hard, then opened her eyes. 'My women', he'd said. Plural. The twist of pain was razor-sharp, but the words had acted like a cold shower. Swallowing convulsively, she found herself nodding slowly.

'I'd like to go to the ballet. And I accept the offer of a spare bed. I'd like us to. . .to spend the evening as. . .as friends.'

'*Friends?*' The soft drawl was teasing, the grey eyes now unreadable. 'How come I didn't get prior warning of a major development in our relationship?'

'Well. . .we're hardly strangers any more, are we?' she demanded, thrusting her hands into her pockets and eyeing him with a trace of annoyance. The atmosphere had cooled down dramatically. Gratitude that she had her errant responses firmly under control was flooding through her. She was almost weak with relief. 'And now

I've confided my murky past, that must make us more than acquaintances.'

'How about business colleagues?' he queried, lifting a quizzical eyebrow. He'd released her, now. A safer distance existed between them. 'Did you come to any decision about those designs?'

'Yes. . .' Not until this very moment, she realised ruefully, flashing him as calm a smile as she could manage. 'I agree. If you really think Chester's could benefit from them, I'd be crazy to refuse, wouldn't I?'

'Absolutely.' The triumph in his eyes was barely contained. 'You won't regret it. . .'

They went to the ballet. The American troupe were refreshingly different, innovative, but Virginia reflected afterwards that she might as well have been watching a film with no pictures, in a language she didn't understand, such was her lack of concentration on the details of that evening.

The simple act of losing herself in a live stage performance seemed impossible, when all she could think of was the sheer heaven of spending time alone with Guy again. There was no logic in it, she scolded herself silently, but logic wasn't always the most important element to be considered. . .

Afterwards, walking along a wet London street and finding an intimate Italian restaurant, eating pizza, sharing a bottle of Frascati, assumed the monumental importance of some banquet at Buckingham Palace. By the time they'd exchanged passionate views on every subject under the sun, from politics to gardening, the supernatural to the world population explosion, she began to suspect she might be coming late to that teenage affliction, blind infatuation.

A chill suddenly struck her, as they left the Aston Martin and took the lift back up to Guy's penthouse apartment. Was this the kind of total immersion in another person which Mortimer Harrison had undergone, in his unhealthy infatuation with her? The parallel sickened her. It wiped the magic sheen off her evening. . .

'Are you OK?' Guy's query was detached, as they pushed the door closed behind them. 'Do you need to ring home, explain where you are?'

'No, it's OK. I told them I might stay with Kit and Teresa. . .'

They stared at each other. Virginia felt horribly self-conscious.

'Take off your coat, Virginia. There's no need to be afraid of me. . .'

She let him help her off with the mackintosh, hang it in the cupboard in the hall.

'Do you have something to sleep in?' Guy's voice was huskier, his gaze travelling the length of her body in the soft floral skirt, white shirt and suede waistcoat. The hunger in his eyes was harnessed, but only just.

'Yes. . . I packed overnight things. . .'

'Do you want a warm drink?' he went on, a wry grin tilting his lips. 'Cocoa? Ovaltine?'

'You'll be asking if I've packed my fleecy nightcap next,' she teased unevenly.

'Go to bed,' he advised grimly, turning away from her. 'You'll find a separate bathroom leading off the spare room. . .'

'Oh. Right. . .goodnight, then.'

'Goodnight, Virginia.' She hesitated, but Guy didn't turn round, and she retreated inside the spare room and pushed the door slowly closed behind her, trying to fight off the dreadful sense of anti-climax. It had been a wonderful evening. Some buried instinct told her that this was not the fitting end. . .

But what did she *want*? Impatience with her own see-saw emotions robbed her of any desire for sleep. She was trembling with tension. After a rapid shower, and a vigorous teeth-cleaning session, she sought her hair-brush and applied her pent-up energy equally vigorously to taming the riotous cloud of curls.

Catching sight of herself in the long wall-mirror as she pulled a peach-coloured, button-necked nightshirt over her head, she found herself wondering what Guy was doing. Abruptly, the sensations she'd felt that night in St Lucia, when they'd come so close to making love, engulfed her with such force that she felt weak at the knees. Bewildered, she slid into bed beneath a vast grey and emerald silk quilt, and lay staring at the patterns of light thrown on the ceiling by the white bedside lamp. But sleep seemed miles away. Sorting her wildly scattered thoughts into some semblance of order seemed far more imperative. . .

She wanted Guy. There, she'd admitted it to herself. Facing the truth brought a tightness to her throat, butterflies to her stomach. But she was frightened of wanting Guy. And it wasn't just because of what happened with Mortimer. . .that was part of it, but the way Guy made her feel, deep inside, must surely mean that any damage done by Mortimer Harrison had been transitory. . .mustn't it?

No, Guy Sterne was just the *wrong* man to want. The sooner she had that timely reminder engraved in foot-high letters somewhere prominent, the safer she'd be. . .

The minutes ticked slowly by. Not since she'd tossed

and turned with a soaring temperature at the start of the glandular fever had she endured such a ghastly night. At three in the morning, she abandoned any hope of getting to sleep. The combination of a strange bed, and a very strange day, she decided, wearily getting up, and debating what to do. A book was what she needed. There was none to be seen in this small guest room, but there'd been shelves of them lining two walls in the sitting-room overlooking the Thames.

She glanced at her tousled appearance in the mirror, and hesitated. She'd travelled light today; she'd packed no dressing gown. The cotton-jersey nightshirt clung to the soft swell of her breasts and closely skimmed the curve of her hips, exposed a great deal of slender tanned thigh. But short of getting dressed, or rummaging in the hall cupboard for her Burberry, or swathing herself in her duvet and sweeping ornaments to the ground as she tiptoed through the sitting-room, she couldn't think of any solution. Anyway, she was surely getting paranoid. She was decent. That was all that mattered. . .and it *was* three o'clock in the morning. She'd probably hear Guy snoring as she passed his bedroom door.

The possibility of discovering that Guy might be human enough to snore lessened her tension considerably. Suppressing a smile, she quietly opened her bedroom door. The hall was in darkness. She pushed open the door to the sitting-room. The room was full of moonlight, skimming in over the river, throwing odd shadows, silvering the monochrome furnishings to a ghostly pallor. Making her way to the bookcase, she was weighing up the possibility of reading the title spines without putting on the light when a table-lamp was clicked on at the other end of the room. She jumped violently, spinning round to see Guy sprawled in an armchair by the window, a half-empty bottle of whisky and a glass on the black marble table beside him.

In a dark olive-green towelling dressing-gown, dark hair ruffled, shadows under his eyes, a pirate-growth of stubble on his jaw, he looked extraordinarily intimidating. Her heart seemed to miss a beat, then began thumping heavily against her ribs.

'I couldn't sleep either. Do you want some whisky?' The glitter in the heavy-lidded gaze wasn't entirely gentle and welcoming, she decided nervously.

'I just came to find a book. . .'

'For the love of God, Virginia, find one and get the hell out of here,' he said with soft violence. He stood up slowly, with just a hint of unsteadiness betraying how much of the whisky he must have drunk. 'I said you could trust me. But if you stand there much longer in that tiny little nightshirt. . .' He stopped abruptly, massaging the back of his neck. 'I'm sorry. But I'm discovering things about myself tonight. Like that there are limits to my self-control. . .'

'Guy. . . I'm frightened. . .' It was an involuntary whisper. She couldn't think why she blurted it out. His eyes narrowed slightly, and the wide mouth twisted in wry apology.

'There's no need to be frightened,' he said wearily. 'What are you frightened of?'

There was a fraught silence. Myself, she wanted to say. I'm frightened of myself. . . She was aware of Guy's presence in every tiny millimetre of her body. Take a grip on yourself, she told herself furiously. But she just stood there, glued to the spot, her stomach in knots, her knees trembling.

'Are you still thinking about that nutcase at the exhibition?' he queried slowly, his expression darkening.

'No.'

The green-grey eyes narrowed on her uncertain expression, and he moved towards her, in a pantherish prowl which made her throat constrict.

'Virginia, if you want us to stay just friends, go now,' he muttered hoarsely, reaching out to circle her upper arms. 'It's the early hours of the morning. My resistance is low. . .'

'I'm going. . .' The whisper was uneven. She began to slowly pull back, but her eyes were trapped in the sudden, melting caress in his gaze.

'In fact, my resistance is non-existent. . .' he groaned tautly, drawing her against him and running his hands down the slim curve of her back, so that their bodies were pressed close together. Thoughts of escape were blotted out, consumed in the liquid fire flowing through her. Involuntarily she slid her own hands around him, caressing the hardness of his shoulders beneath the towelling gown. Reason and caution were dead. She wanted to feel him naked against her, the way he'd felt in St Lucia. She wanted to give herself to Guy Sterne. To hell with logic, and reason and caution. . .

The glitter in his eyes was white-hot as he met her wide-open, startled gaze.

'Guy. . .this is all wrong. . .' Her one last attempt to halt the tide lacked conviction, she knew.

'No. . .it's got to be right. Anything that feels this good has to be right. . .' he said softly, lifting her into his arms and elbowing his way into his bedroom.

His weight against her on the bed was a savage joy. With his towelling gown discarded, Guy's muscular warmth was both alien and familiar in the darkness. The strong fingers peeling the nightshirt upwards, the exploring hunger of the hard mouth on her stomach, her breasts, her lips, it felt as if she'd been waiting for ever for these feelings. . .

Virginia closed her eyes, let the darkness swirl unheeded around her, losing herself utterly in the pleasure of Guy's caresses. Nothing in her life had prepared her for this wanton fire, burning and aching inside her.

'Virginia. . .' Guy's voice was thick with desire against her neck, as she convulsed beneath his stroking fingers. 'Sweetheart, you're so beautiful. . .you've been driving me crazy. . .'

He moved his lips against the sensitive lobe of her ear, then trailed a row of devouring kisses across the high jut of her breasts to the erect peaks of her nipples. She gasped as he took each one in turn inside his mouth, sucking, flicking his tongue over the throbbing tips. When he moved lower, she tangled her fingers in the thick blackness of his hair, shivering as his mouth moved to the intimate core of her sexuality, parting the curled Titian triangle with his tongue. Flashes of glorious reaction exploded through every nerve-ending. A damp heat was building up in her lower body, unbearably tantalising. She was burning all over.

'Touch me, sweetheart. . .' It was a soft growl of passion. Taking her trembling hand downwards, he cupped her fingers around the heavy heat of his sex. 'Tell me you want me, Virginia. . .let me hear you say it, sweetheart. . .'

'I want you.' She hardly recognised her voice. She was

faintly surprised to hear how much it shook, how afraid
she sounded. . . 'I want you, Guy. . .'

'Open your eyes. . .look at me. . .' Her eyelids flew up,
and she stared wide-eyed at the carved steel mask of
Guy's dark face above her. In a split second, she
registered every tiny detail of his appearance, the smooth
texture of his skin above the shadow of beard-growth,
the high cheekbones cast in stark relief in the moonlight.

'I want you. . . I love you. . .' she heard herself
whispering, one detached part of her intellect aghast at
the vulnerable openness of her confession, surprising her
at the same time with the shocking truth. 'God help me,
Guy, I love you. . .'

'Aaah. . . Virginia. . .' Abruptly the heat intensified.
She was trembling uncontrollably beneath him as he
levered her knees wide to accommodate his strength, his
shaft probing the tight, delicate sweetness of her, the
glitter of triumph in his eyes unmistakable even in the
half-light in the bedroom. 'Oh, Virginia. . .'

His convulsive thrust, the sheer unexpected size of the
invasion, at this pinnacle of flayed emotions and raw
honesty, took her entirely by surprise. She cried out,
then the cry caught and choked in her throat. Guy froze,
unmoving, the light and shadow of his face above her
like carved granite. Pinned beneath him, she was shaking
so violently that she had to cling to him to steady herself.

'Virginia. . .sweetheart. . .' The whisper was an
incredulous accusation. 'I didn't realise. . .' With a
shuddering groan, he lowered his damp forehead to rest
on hers, his entire body poised in motionless tension.
'God. . . I swore I wouldn't hurt you. . .'

'It's all right. Please. . .' She was almost inarticulate

with the strange mix of fear, shyness and pure, throbbing
desire. 'Guy. . .don't stop. It's all right. . .'

Without answering, he covered her parted lips with
his own, his tongue entwining with hers in a kiss as deep
and sensitive as his ultimate possession of her body. The
stretched pain in the most secret, intimate part of her
had vanished. In its place, as he at last began to
carefully, cautiously move inside her, came waves of
wondrous, heart-stopping pleasure, so that in the final
seconds before some internal eruption emptied her brain
and dizzied her senses, she gouged her nails unthinkingly
into his back, and wrapped her legs around him in
unthinking, mindless surrender. . .

Either the enormity of the emotional experience, or the
extreme lateness of the hour, or both, acted like a
powerful sedative. Entwined in warm, unconditional
intimacy with Guy's hard body, she slept almost
immediately. How deeply she'd slept she didn't appreciate until she woke to the remote hoot of river traffic, and
the sound of a pigeon cooing rhythmically just outside
the window.

Through the haze of sleep, vague details of last night
began drifting into her mind. When the full, incriminat-
ing replay had reformed in her memory, she opened her
eyes, shivered and stretched, reaching out to feel Guy's
reassuring shape beside her.

The bed was empty. Virginia lay for a few more
seconds, biting her lip and wriggling as each fresh,
lascivious moment relentlessly came back to her. Her
body felt different. Sore, stiff. . . She grimaced ruefully
as she did a swift mental examination and identified

bruises and tender areas which had never before been
either bruised or tender. . .

Last night, she'd told Guy she loved him. That was a
mind-stopping memory. . .it was disturbing enough to
acknowledge it was true. Even more so, to have blurted
it out to him. It felt rather like laying herself in front of
an approaching juggernaut and waiting for the inevitable
annihilation to follow. . .

She sat up, gazing blankly around the big grey and
china-blue bedroom. This was the first time she'd seen
Guy's bedroom in daylight. The décor was still brutally
hard and ultra-modern, but there was a touch more
warmth in this room, she registered slowly. The inner
doors were old pine, the carpet a rich shade of honey-
tan. The duvet she was clutching around her naked body
was a geometric blend of grey and blue. The vast area of
window, visible through vertical hessian blinds, over-
looked the river, like the sitting-room. . .

A scrawled message propped up on the far bedside
table suddenly caught her eye. She couldn't read it from
here. A lurch of painful insecurity made her stare at it
as if it were some small, dangerous animal to approach
with trepidation. She felt too vulnerable, sitting here
naked in bed. If the note was some cryptic escape-route,
if Guy had woken to bitterly regret last night's impulsive
actions. . .

Swinging her legs out of bed, she hunted around for
her nightshirt, flung in a crumpled heap on the carpet,
then studied the piece of paper. Nothing dramatic, no
soul-searching. . . Guy had gone to get a paper, and
some fresh croissants from a nearby bakery. The note
was signed with a 'G', in bold, black ink, and a single
'X' in the corner.

She read it idiotically at least three times, until she'd convinced herself there was no hidden psychological message in the bare statement of fact, and then realised that someone had just come in the front door of the flat and was moving around in the hall.

'Guy. . .?' She felt a curious leap of apprehension at the thought of seeing him again this morning, after the unthinkable intimacy of last night. . . And. . .not shy, exactly. . .what? Exposed. Vulnerable, and exposed. . .

The bedroom door opened, but the questioning smile died slowly on her lips. The new arrival wasn't Guy, but a small, dauntingly slender woman in her late twenties, with almond-shaped blue eyes as bright as diamonds. Thick, immaculately cut ash-blonde hair brushed the padded silk shoulders of a black and white striped Roland Klein suit. She wore impossibly high heels, yet she was still only eye to eye with Virginia in her bare feet. She carried a large black leather Gladstone bag in her hand.

Hard eyes raked Virginia up and down, and the coral-pink mouth curled in bored amusement.

'Well! Good *morning*!' The accent was brittle and precise. 'Oh, dear, I hardly know what to say!'

'I'm afraid Guy's not here right now,' Virginia began as evenly as she could, painfully conscious of the debauched image her tousled appearance must present. 'He's just popped out to buy a paper——'

'And who are you?'

'Virginia Chester.' She held out her hand with determined politeness. The blonde girl ignored the gesture, a gleam coming into her eyes as she examined Virginia with insulting thoroughness.

'Oh, so you're the sexy redhead from Sarah Chester Fabrics. . .'

'I'm the *what*?' Virginia's embarrassment vanished in a surge of incredulous indignation.

'Oh, sorry, it was just something I heard Dad and Guy laughing about the other day. Hi, I'm Nicola Schreider.'

'You're Nicola Schreider. . .?'

At least the blatant rudeness was explained, Virginia thought bleakly. *Laughing* about? Guy had been *laughing* about her, with his business partner?

This was sour grapes, a far-off voice of wisdom suggested. Trouble-stirring from an ex-fiancée? But a dull flush was creeping up her neck, and colouring her cheeks, and she felt furious with herself for the tell-tale signs of insecurity, for the ease with which the other girl had succeeded in humiliating her. . .

With a convulsive swallow, Virginia stared at the beautiful woman who had been Guy's fiancée. Had been? A glance at the tapering elegance of her left hand showed a massive rock of an engagement ring, flashing diamonds on the fourth finger. A sick feeling was beginning in the base of her stomach, growing, filling her with blind misery. *This* was the woman Guy was rumoured to have casually ditched on the reject heap? Nicola Schreider didn't look like the kind of woman any man would ditch. . .

'I just called by to give Guy a message from my father,' the blonde was murmuring, glancing behind her at the half-open front door, then smiling at Virginia with such patent insincerity that she'd have laughed if she hadn't felt like crying her heart out instead. . .

'Dad had dinner with Bertrand Keane of

Farthingdales last night. They're really interested in a buy-out——'

The name of Farthingdales rang several alarm bells. A numb coldness was enveloping her heart. Something was horribly wrong. . .

'Just a minute. . .' Virginia cut across the cool, slightly high-pitched voice, her own low and vibrant with tense fury. '*Who* are Farthingdales interested in buying out? What are you trying to say?'

'I'm not trying to say anything.' The blue eyes glittered very hard in the carefully made-up face. 'I'm just delivering a message, darling! Though, I must admit, I'm surprised you're sleeping with Guy. I'd have thought. . . I mean, conflict of loyalties, you know?'

'No. I don't know.'

Nicola Schreider shrugged small, beautifully proportioned shoulders, and glanced at her watch. 'With Guy selling your family firm to your biggest rival, I'd have thought you *would* know. But then, I'll hand it to Guy— he's *mega*-successful at getting what he wants when he wants it?'

'I don't believe you. . .' It was an automatic response, mechanical. But she was dying inside. There was no other description for this slow, bleeding pain draining her of emotion. 'Guy wouldn't do that. . .he's got plans for the future of Chester's. He's even using designs I did in St Lucia. . .'

'No one wants to buy a dying duck, do they? The more attractive the package, the better the price. Believe what you like. But take a word of advice. . .don't get delusions of grandeur on the basis of a few steamy nights with Guy. . .he's the ultimate bastard where women are concerned, darling. And, since I'm going to marry him, I'm awfully well qualified to judge! *Ciao!*'

CHAPTER NINE

VIRGINIA was zipping up her overnight bag, after a rapid assembly of her belongings, when Guy came back.

'Good morning. . .' The soft warmth in the voice behind her flipped her heart over. She turned slowly to look at him, as he deposited a bag of fragrant croissants and the *Financial Times* carelessly on the hall table and came to lean in the doorway of the guest room. 'I didn't expect to find you up and dressed. . .'

The brilliance of his gaze was almost more than her steeled defences could stand. He must have jogged to the shops and back, she deduced, keeping her brain detached as she stared at him. In a black tracksuit, and well-worn trainers, dark hair tousled, his tanned skin glowing from the exercise, he looked overwhelmingly attractive. She swallowed convulsively, and tightened the belt of her Burberry, turning up the collar as if she was preparing to weather a blizzard before closing numb fingers round the hand-grip of her bag.

'I could hardly travel back to Oxfordshire wearing my skimpy little nightshirt, could I?' she pointed out calmly, taking a brave step towards him. 'Excuse me, would you? I've ordered a taxi. . . I have a train to catch. . .'

Guy's eyes had narrowed, his expression suddenly darkening. There was a charged silence as she waited for him to move.

'Get out of my way, Guy. Please?'

'Virginia. . .' he began, his tone ominously patient. 'Maybe this is an old-fashioned viewpoint, but last night I thought something fairly important went on between the two of us. . .?'

She shook her head so violently that it hurt her neck.

'No. Correction. Last night you got what you wanted and I got what I deserved. I've never suffered fools gladly. I'm not sure how long it'll take me before I can bear to look myself in the mirror again!'

Guy didn't move. He suddenly looked very large and threatening in the doorway. Anger began to mingle with the shuttered coldness in her heart.

'You're not going anywhere until I get an explanation,' he said softly. 'What's going on?'

'Nothing! Nothing is going on! I'm going home, you can get on with your *profligate* lifestyle, marry Nicola Schreider, nip out to St Lucia for sex with the adoring Tara when you get bored, sell off Chester's to Farthingdales and rake in your hefty slice of profit, and then you can go to eternal *hell*, for all I care!'

She was trembling now, rigid with fury, but shaking inside. Her eyes were full of unshed tears, and the effort of holding them back was exhausting.

'Virginia, what the devil are you talking about?' He had his own temper under iron control. The measured ruthlessness of his tone was far more unnerving than an outburst of straightforward anger.

'I'm talking. . . I'm talking about *trust*, and *integrity*, and. . .and *honour*,' she whispered furiously. 'Qualities foreign to your experience!'

'Last night I was thought sufficiently trustworthy to be your first lover.' The cool drawl in Guy's voice was suddenly very much in evidence. 'Your trust appeared so implicit that you didn't even see the need to warn me it was your first time. This morning I rank somewhere beneath paedophiles and muggers of old ladies. Is that it?'

She was white with suppressed emotion now. 'Let me pass, Guy——'

'Not until you come up with some logical reason for all this garbage.'

'You had a visitor while you were gone.' She bit out the words.

Guy clapped a mock-horrified hand to his forehead. 'Hell, not the Vice Squad?'

'Guy this isn't funny!'

'No. It's not funny.' The deliberate mockery had faded from his eyes, and the raw darkness she saw there made her stomach clench in anguish. 'Tell me who this visitor was, Virginia.'

'Your *fiancée*. Nicola Schreider.'

A loaded silence stretched out between them.

'She let herself in. With her own key,' Virginia went on finally, when Guy's taut, mask-like expression appeared to be engraved permanently. 'The diamond on her third finger makes Liz Taylor's look like a bauble from Woolies! Congratulations, you've got *great* taste in engagement rings. . .'

She made to push blindly past him, and to her vague surprise he stood back slowly, and let her pass into the hall, his eyes shuttered, his mouth grim.

'So Nicola came here, and told you we were still engaged?' he questioned quietly. 'What else did Nicola say?'

'She had a message from her father. Your business partner. Bernard Keane of Farthingdales is *very* interested in buying Chester's. One of the "unpleasant changes" in store, is that the way you'd describe it?'

'Virginia. . .'

'Tell me something. . .did you think praising my Caribbean designs would win you an ally in all these underhand schemes of yours? Did you think I'd be so grateful for the chance of a job I wouldn't mind if my family were thrown out of theirs?'

'Virginia——'

A taxi horn sounded below.

'Goodbye, Guy. . . I hope you have a good *laugh* with Nicola and her father next time you see them!'

She grabbed the front door catch, blinded by infuriating tears as she dashed out and slammed the door resoundingly behind her.

She should have known. She should have *known* what it would be like. . . Getting back home to Armscott Manor was a mechanical necessity, but she hardly registered the journey. It whirled by in a blur of faceless people and formless surroundings. Sunk in introspective misery, Virginia couldn't have said later if it was wet or dry, day or night, winter or summer.

Last night had been a cruel joke, she decided, watching the windswept trees and fields of placid cows flash past the train window, without seeing them. The years of being branded impulsive, scatterbrained, too idealistic rushed back to mock her. How, against all the evidence, all the overwhelming knowledge she had about Guy Sterne, could she have let events overtake her like that? How could she have confessed, in that split second of agonised honesty, that she was sufficiently stupid to have fallen in love with him. . .?

Guy was greedy, amoral, obsessed with power and self-gratification. She'd known the kind of man he was. Even if she hadn't, the warnings had been there all along, right from his cavalier mockery in St Lucia, the first moment he saw her. He'd lied about Tara, lied about Nicola Schreider. . .assured her she wasn't his type then pursued her with consummate skill until his ego was satisfied that she was ripe for seduction. . .

She wasn't sure if she groaned out loud, but the middle-aged lady in the opposite seat gave her a worried glance before ducking quickly back into her magazine.

Fury at her own gullibility kept her going until she got home. Then she retreated in bleak anguish to her bedroom, and sat hunched in the window-seat, looking out over the soft rolling lawns and distant Cotswold hills, dimly aware that her single most painful desire was that her mother were still alive, so she could pour out the secret desolation to the one person who'd have understood. . .

'Virgie. . .?'

Lucy's voice was calling her from outside on the landing. With a jolt, Virginia slid stiffly off the window-seat, and glanced at her watch. She'd been sitting motionless for over an hour, conducting an inner battle over the need to alert the board of Chester's about Guy's perfidy, with the stubborn hope that somehow she might be wrong keeping her glued to the spot, torn with indecision. . .

'Virgie. . .!'

Something in Lucy's voice snapped Virginia back to the present. With a deep breath, she opened her bedroom door to see her sister-in-law half standing, half

crouching at the top of the stairs, the perspiring pallor
of her face telling its own alarming story.

'Lucy. . .is it the baby? Oh, Lucy. . .'

On winged feet Virginia was beside her, slipping her
arm beneath Lucy's and round the other girl's back, and
giving her a reassuring hug, 'Come on, come and lie
down in my room; I'll ring Dr Newne. . .'

'No. . .' Lucy gasped, catching her breath, her fingers
digging painfully into Virginia's hand. 'There's no time
for that. . .can you drive me to hospital, Virgie? Right
now?'

'Of course.' Virginia was suddenly as white as her
sister-in-law as they made the tortuous descent down the
wide, dog-leg staircase, and across the hall. 'Just don't
panic. . .you'll be OK, Lucy. . .when did this start?'

'It came on suddenly—Charles has gone to look at
this new sewing-factory equipment at some place in
Wales. . . Dad's playing golf. . . Mrs Chalk's taken the
day off. . .*oh*. . .!'

Lucy's pregnant weight was a daunting burden to
assist across the drive to the Volvo. Virginia was beginning to think they were both going to collapse in a heap,
when the spit of tyres on gravel announced the arrival of
Guy's Aston Martin, skidding to an abrupt halt as he
saw their plight.

Eyes narrowed in concern, he took in the scene
instantly.

'Guy. . .thank God you've come. . .' It was Lucy who
gasped the greeting, through clenched teeth, blue eyes
clouded with fear and pain. 'Oh, Guy. . . I don't want
to lose my baby. . .'

'You're not going to lose your baby, Lucy. . .' The
gentle note of calm certainty in his voice ripped at

Virginia's flayed emotions. With impressive ease he lifted Lucy carefully into the back of his car, and gestured abruptly for Virginia to get in with her.

The short journey was a controlled nightmare. Guy rang ahead to alert the hospital, then rang the factory in Wales to tell Charles. Charles had already left, a couple of hours ago according to the secretary on the other end of the line. Virginia rang Chester's head office, to tell Charles to go straight to the hospital. Then she rang Mrs Chalk, who agreed to curtail her afternoon off to dash back to Armscott, ready to pass on the news if Charles called home first.

'I'm frightened. . . I'm really frightened.' Lucy's voice was a strangled whisper. She looked ashen, her skin shiny with sweat. 'I want Charles with me.'

'Breathe slowly, concentrate on trying to relax. You're going to be fine, Lucy. You and Charles are going to have a beautiful, healthy baby. Just relax. Everything's going to be all right.'

Guy's low voice had a hypnotic quality which had a strangely calming effect on Lucy, but even so Virginia had an appalling fear that everything was going to be far from all right. There was a feverish glaze to Lucy's blue eyes, and her forehead felt far too hot.

They were there at last, Lucy was bundled as gently as speed would allow on to a trolley and whisked off through swing doors, and Virginia stared, hollow-eyed, at Guy as they waited around silently in the reception area. The smell of antiseptic, and the helpless waiting, brought back powerful memories of the visitors' room two years ago, where the doctor had come to break the mind-numbing news that during a routine operation to

remove her appendix her mother had died of heart
failure.

Virginia shivered. She realised that the pain and shock
of that loss had never truly healed. It had shaken her
faith, made her afraid to form deep attachments in case
somehow the pain was repeated. . .

She cast an anguished look at Guy. He'd swopped the
black tracksuit for close-fitting washed-out denims and a
loose crew-neck navy sweatshirt. An extremely battered-
looking tan leather flying-jacket completed the outfit. He
didn't look as if he'd driven down here with business
matters on his mind. . .last night's happenings, even in
this fraught atmosphere, swirled back into her mind to
torment her. . .

'Will Charles get here in time, do you think?' Unbearable anxiety tore the pointless question from her. Guy
couldn't possibly know, any more than she did.

'He may not. But Lucy will cope. She's tougher than
those baby-blue eyes and blonde curls suggest.'

Guy's response was calmly matter-of-fact, but she saw
the tense concern in his eyes. Guy really seemed to care
about Lucy and Charles, she realised distractedly. For
some reason this made his treachery over the company
seem that much greater. Business matters and personal
relationships clearly occupied separate compartments in
Guy's life. But how could he be so. . .*underhand*? How
could he pretend to be planning for Sarah Chester
Fabrics' future, and all the time plotting its demise? It
was what she'd suspected all along, of course. But
somehow over the last twenty-four hours she'd allowed
herself to hope that it wasn't true. And last night. . .she
swallowed convulsively. . .last night she'd felt closer,

physically and spiritually closer to Guy Sterne than to any other person in her whole life. . .

'She'll be all right, Virginia. I know she will. . .'

The urge to throw herself on the tormentingly broad shoulder was too humiliating, and instead she stiffened with fresh anger and resentment towards him.

'How do you know? Just because your father's a doctor?' she queried bitterly, wishing instantly the sneering words hadn't emerged. Guy's expression darkened, and the look he flicked over her was grimly sardonic.

'Crises are supposed to bring out the best in people.'

'I'm sorry. . .' She bit her lip painfully, turning away from his searching eyes. A fraught silence stretched unbearably between them.

'I'll stay,' she said at last. 'There's no need for you to hang around. . .'

'There's every need,' he returned coolly. 'Lucy and Charles are close friends of mine.'

'Unless business interests happen to conflict?' she murmured bitterly.

'I've had a surfeit of your suspicious little mind, Virginia. Guilty until proved innocent, on every count. That's your motto.'

She glared at him, her cheeks flushing with anger. 'You're planning on proving your innocence?' she demanded scornfully.

'I've a feeling I'd be wasting my time. I told you, I'm no saint, Virginia.'

There was a suggestion of the old, mocking Guy in this last retort, but there was an underlying harshness she'd never heard before.

'You're Mrs Chester's sister-in-law?' A nurse had

appeared behind them, and Virginia spun round
quickly.

'Yes. . .how is she?'

'She's in the labour ward, but there may be one or
two complications. It's possible the doctor will opt for a
Caesarian section,' the nurse explained briefly, checking
notes on a clipboard. 'You've contacted Mrs Chester's
husband, I understand?'

'Yes. . .at least, we've left messages. Hopefully he's on
his way.' Virginia's heart seemed to have plummeted
into her stomach. A Caesarian? Wasn't that serious?
Dangerous? Anything could happen under a general
anaesthetic, couldn't it?

Things could go wrong. Things *did* go wrong. . .she'd
trusted in the powers of justice and compassion before,
and she'd lost her mother. . .she'd trusted Mortimer
with her friendship and he'd betrayed her. . .trusted Guy
with the whole of her heart and soul last night and all
the time he'd been laughing behind her back at the 'sexy
redhead' from Chesters. . .

If anything happened to Lucy. . .Virginia's heart
lurched painfully in her chest. Suddenly life seemed
almost unbearably cruel, and fragile and
unpredictable. . .

'Couldn't I see her, before she goes in for surgery?'
Virginia said, her voice low and shaky with emotion.
She was trembling, she dimly realised. Appalled at her
own illogical fear, she couldn't do anything to suppress
it. She could sense Guy watching her with narrowed
attention, and clenched her hands inside the pockets of
her suede waistcoat, battling to get her reactions under
control.

The nurse was shaking her head. 'Sorry, that's out of

the question, I'm afraid. . .we're not even sure surgery
will be necessary. . .'

'Ginny! Guy!' Charles was white-faced, breathless,
rushing towards them. 'I got the message from Mrs
Chalk. . .'

'You're Mrs Lucy Chester's husband?' The nurse
interrupted calmly, 'Just in time, Mr Chester. Your
wife's been asking for you——'

'Charles! Thank God you're here——'

'Here's my car phone number,' Guy cut in evenly.
'You can contact us on that. Come on, Virginia. We'll
go for a drive somewhere, grab some lunch if there's
time. . .'

Before she had time to exchange a word with her
brother, Charles had disappeared through the swing
doors and Virginia found herself hustled, white-faced,
from the hospital and bundled into the Aston Martin. In
shell-shocked silence she sat, huddled in her seat as they
drove away from the hospital.

Guy took the main road out of town, and then turned
off into narrow, winding, leaf-fringed lanes until they
were deep in the unique peace of the Cotswold countryside. Turning off the lane at a sign marked 'Private
Road', they bumped over a long, pot-holed track, climbing up towards the brow of the hill. Stopping by the
warm stone walls of a rambling old thatched farmhouse,
he cut the engine, turning to study her rigid, ashen-faced
tension.

'Why did you march me out like that?' she managed
to whisper eventually. 'I should *be* there. Charles is my
brother——'

'Virginia. . .sweetheart, Lucy will be all right. . .' He
sounded as if the endearment was torn from him. She

was too engulfed with her own bleak terrors to question it.

'If anything happens to Lucy. . .' she whispered raggedly. 'She's such a darling, Guy, and Charles loves her so much. . .'

'I know. And she's going to be all right,' Guy's voice was gently questioning. 'And you're being irrational. . .'

'I know. I'm sorry, I'm not normally hysterical. . .' She made a gigantic effort to pull herself together.

'What is it, Virginia? This isn't just about Lucy and her baby, is it?'

'It's. . .no. My mother went to that hospital for. . .for minor surgery and she *died* and. . .suddenly, just being there, it all came rushing back. . .' She was gabbling again, she distantly realised, but she couldn't seem to help herself, the choked confession wouldn't be suppressed. 'And Lucy's had lots of complications, Guy, it's not a straightforward pregnancy. I'm so *frightened* for her. . .'

'Virginia. . .'

Guy attempted to pull her into his arms, but she resisted, tensing violently against him. He let her go, and to her chagrin she burst into tears. It was no good trying to hold them back. The combined tension and anguish of yesterday and today was suddenly overwhelming.

'You're not just frightened for Lucy. You're grieving all over again for your mother,' Guy suggested finally, his voice deeper. 'That's good, Virginia. Don't be afraid to cry. . .'

She dug blindly in her pocket for a handkerchief, stiffly self-conscious of her fresh lack of control. At least she hadn't cried on his shoulder again. She'd learned a bitter lesson yesterday, she reflected bleakly. He was altogether too expert at drawing confidences. Of all the people in the world to expose her seething mass of fears and insecurities to, Guy Sterne would have been her last choice. . .yet she'd told him about Mortimer, she'd carelessly made him a gift of her virginity, she'd wildly announced she loved him, and now she was baring her soul over the painful anguish of her mother's death. . .

Knowing about Nicola Schreider, knowing about the deal with Farthingdales, here she was sobbing out her troubles to him again, as if he was the most dependable, reassuring bedrock in her life. . .she was mad, she decided dejectedly, she needed locking up. . .

'Did I accuse you of being as hard as nails?' he teased gently, at last, as if reading her mind. 'Beneath that prickly, pessimistic, suspicious shell you're a wreck, Virginia. You need firmly taking in hand.'

She stared stonily out of the windscreen, her brain reeling. The sun had found a chink in the clouds, and was gilding emerald meadows and dark woodlands. A long way off down the hill smoke drifted up from the first stubble-burning of the autumn.

'Virginia. . .your mother's death was tragic. But you can't let it rock your faith in everything else. . .'

'No. I know.' Her voice was stifled.

There was another endless silence.

'Virginia, about last night. . .we have to talk about it——'

'No!' she said intensely, her voice low and fierce. 'I don't want to talk about last night, or about this morning! I'd like to wipe the whole *sordid* episode from my mind, as quickly as possible, if you don't mind, Guy.' She dashed her hand across her eyes, then pressed her knuckles to her mouth in silent misery, determined not to cry again.

'What happened last night wasn't sordid,' he said, his voice taut. 'This morning was the sordid part. Vowing undying love one moment, hurling accustions the next. That's sordid. Lack of trust is the biggest killer in a relationship——'

'We don't *have* a relationship. Don't preach lack of trust at me. I should have stuck with the sense of my own convictions. . .first Tara, then Nicola, then Farthingdales. . . Are you trying to say I should have trusted you over all those. . .those. . .*betrayals*?'

He stared at her for a long, shuttered moment, then wordlessly climbed out of the car and walked slowly round to her door.

'Come on. . .' His tone was surprisingly even. 'I want to show you something.'

He gestured towards the farmhouse, under its cosy mantle of brand new reed thatch, and she gazed at it bleakly. She was in no mood for admiring something so redolent of happy domesticity; the homely welcoming aura surrounding it seemed to sharpen her own unhappiness. There was a small wood behind it, climbing up the slope of the hill, with oak and beech just beginning to turn orange and yellow with autumn colours. There were assorted outhouses, a large pond sporting a couple of Canada geese and some ducks, an orchard behind more stone walls. Apple trees were straining beneath the weight of a bumper crop of what looked like Cox's orange pippins. There was a name, carved into a plate on the wall. 'Millford Crest'.

She glanced coldly up at Guy, very conscious of her swollen eyes and shattered poise.

'You go ahead. I can see all I want to see from here.'

'No, you can't. Come on. . .' He took her arm, and short of starting an undignified fight she saw no option but to join him as he strolled towards the white-painted gate, set in the surrounding outer stone walls. He stared at the house for a long moment, then turned to lean on the gate and gaze down the hillside. The view comprised sheep-filled meadows and the distant stone-tiled roofs of a nearby hamlet.

'Well?' she prompted acidly. 'Is this all you wanted to show me? I'm looking at a farmhouse, some sheep and some hills.'

Guy shook his head slightly, his eyes hardening.

'You're looking at the new owner of Millford Crest. What do you think of the place?'

'Are you saying this is *yours*?'

'All mine,' Guy agreed calmly. 'I exchanged contracts last week. Do you like it?'

She shrugged slightly, for some reason her throat painfully tight again. Why had he bought somewhere here in Oxfordshire? Did he and Nicola Schreider fancy the rural life for a change, while Guy was temporarily involved with carving up Chesters?

'I think a four-wheel-drive might be a good investment.'

'You're right.'

There was a silence.

'Guy, why are you showing me this place?'

'I've started furnishing it. . . I thought you might be interested.'

'Well, I'm not. How many houses do you need, anyway?'

'I'm selling the flat in London.'

'Oh. I see.' She thought of the bleak, futuristic décor and the grey river beneath, and nodded abruptly before other thoughts could crowd unbidden into her head and start that agonised melting all over again. 'You'll have to get Nicola some suitable green wellies,' she suggested nastily. 'She looked like a committed townee to me.'

'She is. I can't see her fitting into a country lifestyle, somehow.'

Something in Guy's voice made her look at him quickly. The light in the pale grey eyes was very bright and hard as he watched her expression.

'In that case it'll be one of those fashionable marriages where the couple live apart most of the time, will it?'

'That kind of marriage wouldn't suit me at all.'

She turned angrily back to the car, but Guy caught up with her in a couple of strides, catching her shoulders, spinning her back to face him.

'Guy. . .' The trembling in her legs had intensified. She had a horrible vision of collapsing in another helpless heap at his feet, and the prospect brought a fresh surge of anger to rescue her. 'I don't want to stay here any longer. I must get back to the hospital. . .'

'They have my car phone number. If anything happens they'll ring. We're ten minutes' drive away at most.'

'I should *be* there. . .'

'Winding yourself up into blind hysteria?' he asked sharply. 'If Charles had hung around long enough to notice the state I saw you in, he'd have thought the worst had happened, Virginia. Now calm down, and listen to me for a minute. I brought you up here because I wanted to show you the house I've bought in Oxfordshire. The house I bought to live in. I'm aware

that you rate my integrity somewhere between that of
Idi Amin and King Rat. I'm not sure why I'm bothering
to try to justify myself. I've a nasty feeling a profiteering
wheeler-dealer like me is never going to be *innocent*
enough for your high-minded ideology. . .'

She was dimly aware that his fingers were biting into
her arms. The brilliance of his gaze was mesmerising.

'Guy, you're *hurting* me——'

The bleep of the carphone shattered the moment of
tension. Abruptly releasing her, Guy strode down to
answer it. Virginia wanted to run after him, but she felt
frozen, riveted to the ground. If it was the hospital, she
realised she was terrified to hear the news. Bad news
had a habit of springing ghastly surprises, the way that
shattering news about her mother had sprung the cruel-
lest surprise of all. . .the way her foolish idyll last night
had been ruthlessly shattered this morning. . .

'We'll be there.' The abrupt response into the telephone broke the spell, brought the adrenalin pounding
through her veins again. Virginia ran urgently down the
hillside to the car. Concern for Lucy and Charles were
suddenly uppermost in her mind again, her own pre-
occupations forgotten.

'What is it? What's happened?'

Guy's mouth twisted into a wry smile, as he saw the
anguished uncertainty in her eyes.

'Lucy's had a baby boy,' he told her, a slight catch in
his voice. 'They're both doing fine.'

'Here's to David Guy Chester, 8 pounds 7 ounces, and
lungs like bellows.' Charles was handing round the silver
tray of champagne, his smile one of pure pleasure and

pride as he gazed round at the assembled family in the conservatory. 'We want you to be godfather, Guy.'

'Bravo. . .' Her father's approval was a jovial rumble as he lifted his glass. 'Excellent idea. . .'

Virginia stared in stunned shock at her brother, and her father. In all the euphoria following the successful birth, and the tea- and sandwich-making with Mrs Chalk afterwards, she'd gone quietly along with everyone's air of respectful gratitude for Guy, who'd saved the day, whisked Lucy to hospital, kept everyone calm and optimistic, loomed in the background like a rock of dependable strength. The announcement that Guy was to be *godfather* to the new baby brought her to her senses with a sharp jolt. She stood up abruptly.

'You want Guy to be godfather?' she echoed incredulously. Bitter fury made her whip around to examine the cool, detached expression in the grey eyes of the offending member of the party. 'Are you crazy? Don't you *realise* what he's doing behind your backs?'

'Ginny, we want you to be David's godmother, too. . .' Charles's beatific smile had only faded a fraction. He was too high on exultant relief to be deflated so easily. Her father was frowning at her over the rim of his glass.

'No sour grapes, please, Virginia. I'm getting rather tired of this vendetta of yours——'

'I heard this morning, through Guy's fiancée Nicola Schreider, that Guy is secretly negotiating with Farthingdales,' she said shakily. 'He's selling Chester's, Dad! So much for all his vague promises of investment and improvement and new product lines. . . We're being sold out to our biggest rivals, just so Schreider Sterne Inc. can clinch another of their famous profitable deals! So do you still want Guy Sterne as your baby's godfather, Charles?'

CHAPTER TEN

CHAMPAGNE glasses frozen in mid-air, Charles and her father exchanged glances, then turned to stare at Guy. There was a charged silence.

Virginia's heart contracted as she watched Guy's narrow-eyed composure. To look at him, propped against the chimney-piece, laconically relaxed in the casual denims and sweatshirt, there was no indication of a man whose cover was blown, whose true colours were revealed. . .

'Is this true, Guy?' Her father spoke first.

'Of course it isn't, Dad,' Charles cut in quickly, shooting a reproving look at Virginia. 'Guy, you'd better explain. Tell them what you were telling me on the phone yesterday. . .'

Guy was looking at Virginia. The grim hostility in his eyes chilled her.

'OK, I'll explain. The negotiations have been secret because they've been. . .controversial. But Farthingdales are not buying Sarah Chester Fabrics. Sarah Chester's is buying Farthingdales——'

'*What*?' Virginia's exclamation was involuntary. 'But that's ridiculous—Chester's hasn't got enough money to buy out a competitor the size of Farthingdales. . .'

Guy's hard gaze remained mask-like. Her accusation in front of her family had made him coldly furious, she realised with a jolt. Suddenly, it was like arguing with an icily detached stranger again. Last night's intimacy

170

seemed doubly incongruous in contrast to this fraught hostility. She balled her fists and fought down the growing desolation inside her.

'It's taken a lot of my notorious skills at wheeling and dealing, but the bank are prepared to finance the deal on the strength of the new patent for the computerised cutting and sewing system,' Guy was saying, his voice flat and clipped. 'Farthingdales are struggling as hard as Chester's in the current market. We buy Farthingdales. We then make the necessary economies and redundancies in *their* company, and save Sarah Chester's neck. It's underhand, but effective. If it upsets Virginia's high-minded principles, that's tough. That's business. . .'

He took a brief drink of champagne, and his mouth twisted in a humourless smile. 'I'm willing to quit a lucrative job in the City for a voyage of discovery in another direction, but only if the set-up I'm quitting for has an even chance of staying afloat for the voyage.'

The ensuing silence seemed to stretch specifically between Guy and Virginia.

'You're planning on staying with Chester's?' Virginia queried at last, her voice shaky. 'You're quitting the City?'

His nod was curt. 'I'm selling my flat, buying the farmhouse I showed you, coming to live here. I like the set-up. Believe it or not, when Charles approached me for help, I saw the attraction of a company specialising in producing beautiful things, which also cares about the people who produce them.'

Virginia recalled her prim lectures in St Lucia, and stared at him in stunned disbelief. The ruthless cynicism in his eyes smote her like a physical blow.

'Guy. . .this morning Nicola said——'

'Nicola came to stir trouble. She found an easy target.'

'Guy, she was wearing your *ring*! She told me you were getting *married*!'

'And you believed it?' Guy shot back softly. 'After last night?'

There was an embarrassed clearing of throats from Charles and her father, who were witnessing the sudden switch of topic with dawning understanding.

'If you'll excuse us. . .' Charles's interjection went unheeded. The quiet closing of the door as the other two men made a tactical retreat was also ignored.

The tension in the room was so high that it flowed like an invisible electric charge.

'Why *shouldn't* I believe it?' Virginia whispered unsteadily, holding Guy's glittering gaze with anguished green eyes. 'It was just like St Lucia again. You told me you and Tara weren't lovers, but the minute you'd left she told me you *were*. There seem to be too many women with very possessive attitudes towards you! Why should I flatter myself I'm special?'

In two long strides, Guy abandoned his leaning position by the fireplace and came to take her by the shoulders, shaking her roughly. His eyes were bright and hostile on her flushed face.

'Get this into your head! First, you *are* special. Second, I am not double-crossing your family behind your back. Third, I am not marrying Nicola Schreider—she's engaged to someone else. Fourth, I slept with Tara *once*, years ago, then finished it because I dislike sex without commitment. Fifth, last night was the most important night of my life so far, and I'd very much like to know if you meant what you said to me when we were making love, Virginia. Because if you did, why in God's name are you so determined not to trust me today?'

Virginia stared at him in tortured uncertainty. His touch seemed to burn her through the thin cotton of her white blouse. She blinked away angry, confused tears, and shook her head slightly.

'Well?' he demanded angrily, his eyes hostile slits in the darkness of his face. 'Did you mean it?'

'What do you want from me?' she said tightly, a catch in her voice. 'Isn't it enough to have two women madly in love with you already? Do you have to add a third scalp to your belt?'

He released his grip on her shoulders, his eyes hardening.

'God, Virginia, what do you want from *me*?' he ground out ferociously. 'If you want some fairy-tale knight on a white charger, forget it! I'm human, I'm fallible, I'm thirty-two years old, I've got a past. There's nothing I can do about that!'

'Guy. . .please. . .' The words were a strangled whisper. The violence in him was suddenly frightening, yet it touched her inside, caught her up in a tangle of emotions too powerful to analyse.

'All that trust, and honour and integrity you preach about—the last two you might have a surfeit of, but the first one? If you're sitting in judgement on every wrecked relationship from my past, I'm fighting a losing battle with you all the way down the line!'

She stared at the fierce pain in his eyes, her heart thudding dully in her chest. 'Guy, I just don't know how to handle the way I feel. . .' It was a half-sob. She wanted to fling herself into his arms, but the cold fury she saw in his face kept her riveted to the spot. 'I need time to think. . .'

There was an agonised silence. They stared at each other, ashen-faced, grey eyes locked bleakly with green.

'Sure. . .' Guy moved first, reaching to briefly touch her face then dropping his hand wearily to his side. 'You've got it. You can have all the time in the world, Virginia. . .'

The words were bitter, cynically mocking. In choked desolation, she watched him walk quietly to the door and let himself out. The front door slammed distantly, the Aston Martin's tyres scattered the gravel noisily on the drive, and still she stood there, torn inside, unmoving, until Charles came to see if she was coming with them to the hospital to visit Lucy.

'Don't you just adore him, Virgie?' Lucy was propped on pillows in the narrow hospital bed, holding the tiny night-gowned bundle in the crook of her arm. She brushed loving fingers over the wisps of dark hair clearly inherited from Charles. Her smile was radiant.

'He's gorgeous, Lucy,' Virginia said quietly. 'He's got your blue eyes. . .'

'I just can't believe it's all over. . .'

'When David Guy Chester made up his mind to come into the world there was no stopping him.' Charles grinned, leaning over Lucy's shoulder to tickle his son under the chin. 'He looks a bit like Dad, don't you think, Ginny?'

'Sorry?'

'Virginia's got other things on her mind,' said her father, with a thoughtful glance in his daughter's direction. Her white-faced preoccupation suddenly drew everyone's interest, and she winced inwardly as Lucy suddenly frowned.

'Where's Guy, by the way? Charles and I want him to be godfather, did Charles say?'

'Yes. Charles said.'

There was a slightly awkward silence.

'What is it?' Lucy queried curiously, looking from one to another. 'What's wrong?'

'Guy and Virginia had a. . .difference of opinion,' Charles supplied cautiously.

'I'm afraid I caused a bit of a scene. . .' Virginia confessed miserably. 'I accused Guy of selling off Chester's to our rivals, but it appears he was planning the opposite. . .'

She was slowly dying inside, she decided despairingly. She'd driven a wedge between herself and Guy. He'd abruptly become so distant, so. . .uninterested. Was that what she wanted? Lack of trust was the killer in relationships, he'd said earlier. Was that what she'd done? Killed whatever Guy might have felt for her?

'Then the argument got decidedly personal,' Charles added, 'so Dad and I beat a hasty retreat!'

Lucy was staring intently at Virginia, her eyes glinting with interest. 'Personal in what way?' she queried gently, fixing Virginia with a look it was hard to evade. 'What's been going on between you and Guy, Virgie, darling? I've been hoping against hope you two would get together!'

'We did, briefly, last night,' Virginia admitted bitterly, colouring slightly at her father's sharp glance. 'It's OK, Dad. I am twenty-one, over the age of consent.'

'I'm well aware of that, my dear.' Her father's reaction

was remarkably mild. Virginia caught her lip between her teeth, managed a rueful smile.

'Sorry. . . I didn't mean to snap. . .'

'You two. . .' Lucy waved an imperious hand at her husband and her father-in-law. 'Scat! I want to talk to Virgie! Now,' she prompted, when with much protesting her order had been obeyed, 'tell me all about it!'

Unburdening herself to her sister-in-law proved strangely cathartic, Virginia thought, as she haltingly finished a pared-down version of recent events, leaving out Mortimer, and a great deal of strictly private information besides.

'It's true about Nicola Schreider,' Lucy confirmed, at length, rocking her baby son backwards and forwards as he showed signs of exercising the excellent lungs Charles had described. 'I heard from a friend this morning— she'd getting hitched to some chap in Northamptonshire who's due to inherit his uncle's title.'

'Then why did she lie to me?'

'Dog in the manger?' Lucy suggested wryly. 'She can't have Guy, so no one else should either?'

'Guy seems to change his women the way he changes his socks,' Virginia muttered acidly, her heart aching.

Lucy's gaze was very direct. 'You're in love with him, and I'll lay odds he's besotted with you. I've seen the way he looks at you, Virgie! I think you'll find all Guy needs is the right woman.'

'I'm not sure I could stand the pain if I found myself being exchanged for a newer model!' Virginia confessed in wry anguish. 'I've never felt like this about anyone, Lucy! He makes me feel so. . .horribly vulnerable. . .'

'There are no guarantees to happiness, Virgie, darling!

But Guy Sterne is one of the nicest men I know. If you want him, stake your claim. That's my advice.'

David Chester chose that moment to demonstrate his lung capacity, and the confidences were abruptly ended. But, while she was driving home, Lucy's advice echoed round her head. Virginia found herself desperately hoping Guy would be back at Armscott Manor, because suddenly she was possessed with a burning need to talk to him, build some kind of bridge over the chasm she'd caused with her accusation over Farthingdales.

He hadn't been back, Mrs Chalk assured her, as she prepared to serve a light cheese and fruit supper. And no, he hadn't rung. Virginia went up to her bedroom with a heavy heart, to change out of the clothes she'd worn all day. After a hasty shower, she chose pleat-waisted tan cords and a cream checked shirt, knotted a thick Aran sweater round her neck and brushed her hair with suppressed violence until it shone in a red-gold cloud down her back. Maybe when she got back down-stairs Guy would be there. . .

He wasn't. The plummeting of her heart did more to convince her of her true feelings than any rational thinking. She wanted to see him so badly that she felt physically bereft. The things he'd said, the things she'd said. . .it had all gone round and round inside her head a hundred times. She *had* to talk to him. . .

She couldn't eat any supper. Excusing herself from the table, she found Guy's London number in the telephone book and dialled it in the privacy of the study. She imagined the telephone tone bleeping out in the iron-grey sitting-room overlooking the Thames, her fist gripping the receiver so tightly that her knuckles were white. There was no reply. She'd assumed he'd driven

back to London, but maybe he hadn't. Maybe he was
still in Oxfordshire? Another thought struck her—the
farmhouse he'd taken her to see that morning. . .could
he have gone there? Gone to Millford Crest?

With a brief announcement that she was going out,
she grabbed a waxed jacket from the hall and ran out to
the Volvo, her stomach in knots as she unlocked the
door. The September evening was already growing dark.
Woodsmoke and the pungent aroma of apples and
Michaelmas daisies spiced the dusk. She thought of St
Lucia, of the dark tropical evenings with their different
heady mix of spicy perfumes carried on the trade winds,
and her heart ached unbearably as she followed the
winding country lanes to the small, bumpy track marked
'Private Road'.

Then her heart stopped aching and did a painful jerk.
The Aston Martin was parked outside the white gates.
There was a light on in one of the downstairs rooms.
Guy was here.

The wind was cool, and the night was now pitch dark
as she made her way slowly to the front door. On her
way, she passed the room with the light on, and she
looked in with a stab of surprised longing at the cosy
scene inside. If Guy had only exchanged contracts last
week, he'd organised himself with impressive speed.

A log fire burned in the hearth, there was a huge
Persian rug on mellow oak-block flooring, three high-
backed sofas, traditional two-seaters but covered in a
soft paprika-coloured corduroy instead of the usual
chintz. There was a beautiful walnut kneehole desk in
an alcove, with a file of papers strewn open, and a half-
empty glass of what looked like red wine standing there.
There was no sign of Guy.

Feeling ridiculously nervous, she knocked on the door and waited, but no one came. She knocked again, then pushed the door and found it unlocked. The light in the room with the desk drew her inside. She wanted to call out to Guy to tell him she was here, but somehow her voice seemed stuck in her throat and she couldn't bring herself to do it.

Instead she went towards the fire, and slowly sat down on one of the corduroy sofas. It seemed a long time before footsteps came along the hall, the door was pushed wider and Guy appeared with an armful of logs.

He stared at her in silence for an agonising time, grey eyes heavy-lidded, the expression in their depths unreadable.

'Well, well. Goldilocks, I presume?' The flat drawl was so calmly unmoved that she felt her throat dry in panic. What *was* she doing here? She'd asked for time, hadn't she? Guy had appeared quite happy to grant her all she needed. She'd had all of four or five hours, before she'd come rushing after him like a lovelorn schoolgirl. . .

'As in, "look who's sitting in my chair"?' she echoed shakily, remembering the way Guy had reacted that unforgettable night in St Lucia.

Guy shouldered his way through the door and dumped the logs unceremoniously in the log basket, straightening to brush the splinters from his sweatshirt. His glance at her was unfathomable. He checked his watch, raising an eyebrow.

'It's ten o'clock, Virginia. I was planning on an early night. I assume there's a specific reason for this surprise visit?'

'Guy, will you stop being so. . .*cool*, and detached, and. . .*cynical*?' she said, her voice low and intense.

'How would you like me to be?' he queried coolly. 'Dead drunk to ease frustration? Dying slowly of a broken heart?'

The casual cruelty of his words cut her like a knife. White-faced, too shocked for tears, she rose slowly to her feet. It was now or never, she realised numbly. Lucy's advice rang in her ears. But it was more than that. Her emotions seemed to have undergone a deep sea-change over the last few hours. From fearing that a total commitment to Guy Sterne would be the greatest mistake of her life, for some inexplicable reason she couldn't now seem to envisage a future without him. Admitting that to someone as detached and uninterested as the man standing in front of the fireplace was going to take all the courage she had. . .

'What do you want, Virginia?' His eyes were very hard beneath the heavy lids. She caught her breath in abrupt panic, colour washing over her face.

'You,' she told him shakily. 'I want you, Guy.'

His harsh gaze didn't falter.

'I was under the impression you'd had me,' he drawled, the ruthless mockery stronger. 'And found too many imperfections.'

She closed her eyes abruptly, trying to blot out that glitter of derision. This was purgatory, worse than anything she'd faced in her life.

When she opened her eyes again, Guy hadn't moved. She swallowed convulsively, steeling herself against the humiliation of exposing her true feelings.

'That's not how it is. . . Guy, I'm not feeling proud of myself tonight. I've been. . .self-righteous, suspicious. . .what's more, I'm an appalling coward. If you've got any imperfections I've got twice as many. . .'

'Stop it, Virginia. . .' Guy's voice was harsh, the taut mask of detachment crumbling as she stared at him in bleak misery.

'I *did* mean what I said last night,' she went on in a strangled whisper. 'I'm sorry I didn't trust you, and I do love you, Guy. . .'

He muttered something unrepeatable under his breath and wiped an exhausted hand upwards over his forehead, a distraught gesture which ruffled the short dark hair so that it stood on end.

'Will you stop this?' he repeated hoarsely. 'Stop bloody apologising, Virginia? And come here?'

She stared at him blankly, the numb feeling increasing. Feeling like a player on a stage, disconnected with reality, she took a step towards him, her fingernails digging into her palms, a sick ache in her stomach. It was too late, she'd accused him once too often, preached one too many sermons. . .she'd blown her chance to get close to Guy. He was an expert at extracting himself from emotional entanglements. . .the bitter voices were mocking her. . .

'Look, I'm sorry. . .' she managed to say huskily, forcing a tight smile while she died a thousand deaths inside. 'I didn't mean to embarrass you, Guy. . .it's just that I thought. . . I mean I wasn't sure how things stood. . .'

'*Embarrass* me?' He closed the two feet separating them in one angry stride and caught her white face between his hands, his gaze savage, 'You think hearing you say you love me *embarrasses* me?'

'I don't know,' she whispered chokingly. 'Tell me how it makes you feel?'

His fingers thrust shakily up into her hair, held her

head still. He kissed her with suppressed violence, then let her go so abruptly that she almost lost balance.

'I doubt if there are words to describe how it makes me feel,' he told her with a glimmer of the wry mockery back in his eyes. 'Just don't do any more apologising. Hearing you apologise for the things I love most about you is more than I can stand!'

'Oh, Guy. . .!' The joy creeping through her was gradually healing her battered emotions. '*Do* you love me?'

He stood very still for a few seconds, a faint frown lining his forehead, then the wide mouth twisted in the wry teasing smile which flipped her heart over.

'Put it like this: if you ever leave me I'll probably commit hara-kiri with a blunt penknife.'

'Guy!' She shuddered, half laughing, the joy reaching her heart and enveloping her in such a wave of pleasure that she felt weak-kneed. 'That's a *horrible* thing to say!'

'It would be a horrible thing to do. The remedy is not to leave me.'

'Guy. . .' She breathed his name on a husky smile as he trapped her in his arms and covered her parted lips with his mouth. The volatile combination of passion and laughter was so overwhelming that Virginia shut her eyes and tangled her fingers in the ruffled dark hair and began to drown in the exquisite taste and texture and sensation of kissing Guy and being kissed back very comprehensively in return.

It was a long time before Guy released his fierce hold on her, and reluctantly thrust her away from him. She stared into his eyes, and saw the suppressed hunger there, and her heart seemed to contract then swell inside her.

'I have to talk to you about Nicola. . .' he murmured raggedly, the look in his eyes melting her stomach. 'I never loved her, Virginia. And I doubt if she ever loved me. . .'

Virginia blinked at him, shook her head slightly. 'It doesn't matter, Guy. You don't have to explain. . .'

'Yes, I do. Getting engaged to marry someone, then breaking it off—that's a serious mistake. I need to explain. . .' His voice was a fraction harsher, his eyes steady on hers. He steered her to the sofa, drew her down beside him.

'I'll keep this brief. . . I'm not proud of any of it. Joseph Schreider was a kind of. . .surrogate father. Power and wealth were natural goals for him. He didn't despise the concepts the way my parents did. His daughter Nicola came back from her expensive Swiss finishing-school and decided she liked the look of me. She looked good, she was quite good fun to be with, it made good business sense. . . Neither of us were thinking too deeply. I was on a kind of. . .half-throttle, emotionally. The crunch came when I found out she was sleeping with a couple of other boyfriends, and I discovered I didn't actually *care*. That's when I woke up to the fact that there was something very wrong with the relationship, and very wrong with my life. . .'

Guy broke off, his glance at her surprisingly wary and diffident.

'This is your cue for some moralistic preaching,' he prompted, with a slightly shaky grin. In answer, she tightened her arms round him, shook her head determinedly.

'No way. I shall never preach at you again. I don't

mind your rakish past as long as you're a genuinely reformed character!' she teased unsteadily.

'You are looking at a genuinely reformed character,' he assured her with soft intensity, his gaze darkening as his eyes roved hungrily over her flushed cheeks, then down to the open neck of her checked blouse where her breasts were crushed against his chest. 'Do you want to know about Tara?'

'No!'

'She's decided to take her limbo dancing skills to Jamaica,' Guy told her relentlessly. 'She's left St Lucia. Noble Soloman's sister Malika has taken over her job. . . Virginia, will you marry me?'

The question caught her by surprise. The colour heightened then receded in her face, and she released him, sat back, startled.

'Yes, of course I will,' she whispered at last, her pulses racing idiotically fast.

'Next week, by special licence?' Guy's gaze was narrowed again, harder to read.

'I. . .yes! But. . .well, shouldn't we wait a bit longer? Make quite sure it's what we both want. . .?' The tentative protest was cut short as she was abruptly flattened along the sofa, pinned mercilessly beneath him.

'Just tell me. . .is it what *you* want?' he demanded with soft violence.

'Yes! More than anything. . .yes! But when did you. . . I mean, how long have you. . .?' She was scarlet with confusion, the breathtaking desire mounting between them making it difficult to cling to her train of thought.

'How long have I wanted to marry you?' Guy supplied grimly, dropping a possessive kiss on her mouth, 'Since I arrived in St Lucia for a spell of solitary soul-searching, and an evil-tempered harpy with a mop of red hair and no clothes on leapt off my bed and started calling me rude names. . .'

'Evil-tempered *harpy*?' she protested weakly. 'That's a bit strong. . .'

'By the time you'd ripped my character to shreds, lectured me on my grasping capitalist principles, then forced yourself to be nice to me out of commendable loyalty to your family firm, I was hooked. I'm a masochist, Virginia. Marrying you will be a welcome alternative to a lifetime of self-flagellation——'

With a muffled shriek, she pushed at his weight with her hands and knees, half laughing as he squashed her flat again and controlled her flailing arms with a glitter of laughter in his eyes.

'You'll be bitterly disappointed,' she warned him, her eyes dancing. 'I'm so besotted with you, I'll probably love, honour and obey with depressing servitude!'

'I'll take the risk!' he groaned, lowering his mouth to the base of her neck and sliding his hands along the soft pliancy of her body with such a startling response that further dissent was impossible.

'I can't believe it's nearly October.' Virginia turned her head lazily where she lay supine on the fine white sand, and shot Guy a smile of such radiance that he flipped off his Raybans and propped himself on his elbows to scrutinise her more intently. They'd swum and picnicked, and now they were lying in the shade of a drunkenly angled coconut palm, and all around them the sun glistened relentlessly on sapphire water and brilliant green vegetation.

'It's raining in Oxfordshire,' he agreed, his lips tilting at her sybaritic contentment.

'There's something terribly. . .*decadent* about lazing in the Caribbean when it's raining in England,' she murmured.

'Almost as decadent as the new Mrs Guy Sterne,' Guy drawled teasingly, 'whose boundless enthusiasm for creative design in her new role as director of Chester's Mother and Child subsidiary is exceeded only by her boundless enthusiasm for the more *physical* aspects of her new role as the new Mrs Guy Sterne. . .*ouch*!'

He reeled under the well-aimed punch, and then snaked an arm out to haul her over to his towel, pinning her down with one muscular leg.

'It's no use denying it,' he breathed against her ear, as she squirmed to get free. 'I've scarcely seen daylight since we arrived. . .'

'The only reason we've spent so much time making love is to stop me talking about business,' she complained with an unabashed grin.

'Rubbish. You can discuss business any time you like, as long as you don't start moralising about the redundancies in Farthingdales. . .'

'I'm not *moralising*,' she began earnestly. 'I just keep wondering if there's another way of approaching the problem. . .'

'See what I mean?'

'At least I know how to get you to kiss me,' she provoked softly. 'And anyway, are you complaining?' She was half laughing, half melting under the determined onslaught of his caresses. 'Can I help it if your debauched skills have turned me into a. . .a strumpet?'

'A *what*?'

'A strumpet. . .that's a lewd, wanton, unchaste woman who——'

'Yes, I do know the dictionary definition of strumpet, and I love it when you talk dirty,' he growled, his eyes glittering with wicked amusement. 'But I rather think my modest, high-minded, fastidious, idealistic wife has a long way to go before she qualifies for that description.'

'Really? I thought I was getting the hang of it quite well!' Her eyes were exultantly brazen as she stared up at him.

'Not bad for a beginner,' he allowed huskily. 'But if you want concessions on the Farthingdales take-over, I'd say there's undoubtedly room for improvement!'

'Guy. . .that's *unworthy* of you!' she chided shakily, 'And we can't possibly. . .not here. . . Guy, we can't do that *here*. . .!'

Her turquoise swimsuit was already being remorselessly dispensed with, and as further protests were silenced by Guy's laughing mouth covering hers, and her writhing body was explored by his skilful fingers, the laughter was replaced by something much more urgent and potent, as Guy tossed the clinging garment aside, and spread-eagled his wife with breathtaking impatience across the towel, proceeding to demonstrate an audacious variation on what promised to be another perfectly designed performance. . .

Mills & Boon

Next month's Romances

Each month, you can choose from a world of variety in romance with Mills & Boon. These are the new titles to look out for next month.

SUMMER STORMS Emma Goldrick

PAST PASSION Penny Jordan

FORBIDDEN FRUIT Charlotte Lamb

BAD NEIGHBOURS Jessica Steele

AN UNUSUAL AFFAIR Lindsay Armstrong

WILD STREAK Kay Thorpe

WIFE FOR A NIGHT Angela Devine

WEEKEND WIFE Sue Peters

DEAR MISS JONES Catherine Spencer

CLOAK OF DARKNESS Sara Wood

A MATCH FOR MEREDITH Jenny Arden

WINTER CHALLENGE Rachel Elliot

CASTLE OF DESIRE Sally Heywood

CERTAIN OF NOTHING Rosemary Carter

TO TRUST MY LOVE Sandra Field

STARSIGN

SHADOW ON THE SEA Helena Dawson

Available from Boots, Martins, John Menzies, W.H. Smith, most supermarkets and other paperback stockists.

Also available from Mills and Boon Reader Service, P.O. Box 236, Thornton Road, Croydon, Surrey CR9 3RU.

From the author of Mirrors comes an enchanting romance

PATRICIA MATTHEWS

Caught in the steamy heat of America's New South, Rebecca Trenton finds herself torn between two brothers – she yearns for one, but a dark secret binds her to the other.

Off the coast of South Carolina lay Pirate's Bank – a small island as intriguing as the legendary family that lived there. As the mystery surrounding the island deepened, so Rebecca was drawn further into the family's dark secret – and only one man's love could save her from the treachery which now threatened her life.

W●RLDWIDE

4 FREE

Romances and 2 FREE gifts just for you!

You can enjoy all the heartwarming emotion of true love for FREE! Discover the heartbreak and the happiness, the emotion and the tenderness of the modern relationships in Mills & Boon Romances.

We'll send you 4 captivating Romances as a special offer from Mills & Boon Reader Service, along with the chance to have 6 Romances delivered to your door each month.

Claim your FREE books and gifts overleaf...

An irresistible offer from Mills & Boon

Here's a personal invitation from Mills & Boon Reader Service, to become a regular reader of Romances. To welcome you, we'd like you to have 4 books, a CUDDLY TEDDY and a special MYSTERY GIFT absolutely FREE.

Then you could look forward each month to receiving 6 brand new Romances, delivered to your door, postage and packing free! Plus our free newsletter featuring author news, competitions, special offers and much more.

This invitation comes with no strings attached. You may cancel or suspend your subscription at any time, and still keep your free books and gifts.

It's so easy. Send no money now. Simply fill in the coupon below and post it to -
Reader Service, FREEPOST, PO Box 236, Croydon, Surrey CR9 9EL.

- - - - - - - - - NO STAMP REQUIRED - - - - - - - - -

Free Books Coupon

Yes! Please rush me my 4 free Romances and 2 free gifts! Please also reserve me a Reader Service subscription. If I decide to subscribe I can look forward to receiving 6 brand new Romances each month for just £9.60, postage and packing free. If I choose not to subscribe I shall write to you within 10 days - I can keep the books and gifts whatever I decide. I may cancel or suspend my subscription at any time. I am over 18 years of age.

Name Mrs/Miss/Ms/Mr _____ EP18R

Address _____

_____

Postcode _____ Signature _____